SPECIAL MESSAGE TO READERS

This book is published by

THE ULVERSCROFT FOUNDATION

a registered charity in the U.K., No. 264873

The Foundation was established in 1974 to provide funds to help towards research, diagnosis and treatment of eye diseases. Below are a few examples of contributions made by THE ULVERSCROFT FOUNDATION:

A new Children's Assessment Unit at Moorfield's Hospital, London.

•

Twin operating theatres at the Western Ophthalmic Hospital, London.

•

The Frederick Thorpe Ulverscroft Chair of Ophthalmology at the University of Leicester.

•

Eye Laser equipment to various eye hospitals.

If you would like to help further the work of the Foundation by making a donation or leaving a legacy, every contribution, no matter how small, is received with gratitude. Please write for details to:

THE ULVERSCROFT FOUNDATION,
The Green, Bradgate Road, Anstey,
Leicester LE7 7FU. England
Telephone: (0533)364325

THE GOLD MOVERS

Only in Cooper City, far east of his claim, could the old prospector find a bank vault big enough to store his gold. It had taken Coote and his niece many years to mine it — the Ortner gang could seize it in minutes. With the Texas trouble-shooters riding escort, the ambushers would have to do it the hard way.

MARSHALL GROVER

THE GOLD MOVERS

A Larry & Stretch Western

Complete and Unabridged

LINFORD
Leicester

First published in Australia in 1990 by
Horwitz Grahame Pty Limited
Australia

First Linford Edition
published June 1994
by arrangement with
Horwitz Grahame Pty Limited
Australia

British Library CIP Data

Grover, Marshall
Larry & Stretch: the gold movers.
—Large print ed.—
Linford western library
I. Title II. Series
823 [F]

ISBN 0–7089–7577–1

Published by
F. A. Thorpe (Publishing) Ltd.
Anstey, Leicestershire

Set by Words & Graphics Ltd.
Anstey, Leicestershire
Printed and bound in Great Britain by
T. J. Press (Padstow) Ltd., Padstow, Cornwall

This book is printed on acid-free paper

1

Right Place, Right Time

THEY were at peace with the world, but their names were Valentine and Emerson so, for them, peace was a temporary respite. Tall, Texan and nomadic, they strolled the main street of the town they had found around noon of this day — Tyson, Colorado, a mining town quieter than most. Their horses were stabled, they had rented rooms at a hotel and enjoyed a hearty lunch.

Larry Valentine and Woodville 'Stretch' Emerson, the Lone Star hellions known to the law, the lawless and the frontier press as the Texas Trouble-Shooters, were financially comfortable at this time and hoping their stay in Tyson would be commotion-free.

A female voice, loud and cheery, compelled them to pause on a corner and study a rider entering the street from the north.

"Salted venison! Plucked quail! Jack-rabbits skinned and gutted and fresh! Who'll buy?"

She appeared to the veteran adventurers pathetically young, seventeen at most. Her auburn hair was cut short. The face was pretty with a faint sprinkle of freckles. She was shabbily garbed in Levis, flannel shirt and frayed denim jacket, a floppy-brimmed felt hat planted on the back of her head. Her mount was a smart-stepping black filly. She led a plodding mule toting the meat she offered for sale, and hotel cooks, cafe owners and other townfolk were already converging on her to make their bids. Plainly, she was a familiar figure in this territory.

The tall strangers were intrigued and the grey-haired, black-suited local pausing beside them read their minds.

"Oblige me with a light and, in return, I'll satisfy your curiosity about Mary Kate Feeney," he offered.

They turned to appraise the elder citizen who had filled his brier pipe and needed a match. As Larry obliged him, he looked them over and assumed them to be drifting cowhands and little more. Which proved how wrong Dr. Dana Arledge could be.

True, range clothes were their favorite garb, they having been born and raised in Texas cattle country. True, they did sign on as ranch-hands when their joint bankroll became thin. Or horse-breakers, railroad track-layers, escort riders on gold or payroll shipments or any other chores by which they could earn an honest dollar. But mostly they drifted, gambled and locked horns with denizens of the outlaw trails. They had, in fact, captured more bandidos, slain more desperadoes in mortal combat than any lawman west of the Mississippi could tally. The joke was on them. They hadn't planned on becoming outlaw-fighters of considerable notoriety when quitting their homestate long years before, but it happened anyway. Try as they might, they seemed incapable of dodging conflict with the lawless.

The medico got his pipe drawing to his satisfaction and talked of the enterprising Mary Kate.

"Lives with her uncle, her only relative, at his claim in the high country north. Cosmo Coote's no luckier than most of his kind. Chances are he'll never strike it rich. But he and his niece have their pride, never yet begged a handout. When they're short on provisions, they hunt game. She fetches it to town to trade or sell. That's how they keep going. Nice kid, Mary Kate, barely a day over seventeen. Everybody admires her."

"Everybody ought to," opined sentimental Stretch. The taller drifter was homely with unruly blond hair, jug-handle ears and a lantern jaw; he stood six and a half feet bootless, which made him three inches taller than his brawny partner. "Winchester pokin' out of her saddle-scabbard. She shares the huntin' chores, huh?"

"I bet she's smart with that long gun," said dark-haired, ruggedly-handsome Larry.

"You'd win that bet," nodded Arledge.

He exchanged a few pleasantries with the strangers and continued on his way. They stayed on the corner, building and lighting cigarettes of Bull Durham, smoking and watching the trim-figured redhead unload everything the mule toted, then head for local stores to buy provisions.

They forgot Mary Kate Feeney, took it for granted she had returned to her uncle's claim, until after supper that evening. They were strolling again. There was clear moonlight and a chill in the air and they were passing an alley-mouth, about to cross the street to patronize a saloon, when the faint but audible sound brought them to a halt. It had sounded like a choked off cry for help.

"Down back of this alley," frowned Larry.

"So what're we waitin' for?" demanded Stretch.

A superflous question. They were moving already and fast, bounding into the alley and on to the decaying structure at its rear end, an abandoned barn. The sound was repeated, this time an unladylike curse, and was followed by a gasp of pain and an obscene oath, two other voices, both male.

The tall men charged in with so much moonlight shafting through gaps in the plank walls that they could take in the ugly scene in one quick glance, the girl half-prone, her flannel shirt torn, her shoulders bare, the man with the scratched face aiming a blow at her, the other gripping her ankles. Irate, the Texans descended on them to wreak havoc.

Larry grappled with the man clawed

by the intended victim. The girl rolled clear as Stretch hauled the other rogue upright and slammed three punishing blows to his mid-section. Winded, the man began sagging and, mercilessly, Stretch unwound an uppercut that threw him against a side wall. Dislodged planks clattered and Stretch wasn't through with his yet. Again, he hauled him upright, keeping him up with his right hand while pounding at his ribs with his bunched left. Strong men attacking females of any age were not high on Stretch's list of heroes of the west.

And that went double for Larry, now beating hell out of the first would-be rapist, a hefty hard case whose efforts to defend himself were futile, so hard and fast were the blows Larry rained on him. He was completely unconscious when he began collapsing, and Larry was still punching.

As well as being grateful, Mary Kate Feeney was profoundly impressed.

"Holy Moses," she breathed. "You

sure worked hard at hurtin' them grabbers."

They stood over the senseless duo, breathing heavily, still furious. Larry unclenched his fist, drew a sleeve over his face and muttered. "Question is, Mary Kate, did *they* get to hurt *you*?"

She was fumbling to resecure her shirt, squinting up at her rescuers.

"Slapped me around after they dragged me in here, tore my blouse," she mumbled. "You must've heard me holler, so that's all the hurtin' I took. But I ain't stupid. I know what they *meant* to do to me — so I'm mighty obliged." She found her hat, tugged it on and got to her feet. "What do we do with 'em now? Ain't fair they should get away with this."

"That's puttin' it mild, honey," said Stretch.

"Sheriff's office — downtown, I think," Larry said as he hauled his man upright and draped him over his shoulders.

"Sheriff Hill," she nodded. "We'll

likely find him all by himself. He's got a deputy, fat feller called Tub Mooney, but he keeps sneakin' up to the mountains with a pickax, got the gold fever."

"You feel up to swearin' a statement, a charge?" asked Larry. "That's what the sheriff'll need."

Again she was impressed; he seemed oblivious to the weight of the rogue hung across his shoulders.

"You betcha," she said.

"Bueno," grunted Stretch, picking up the other hard case. "Lead the way, Mary Kate."

As they quit the rotting building and the side alley, she thought to ask, "How come you know my name?"

"Old gent told us," said Stretch. "We saw you bring your tradin' goods in. My partner's Lawrence. I'm Woodville."

Nothing more was said until they entered the clapboard office fronting the jail and let their burdens thud to the floor. A balding, scrawny man rose from a sagging couch, his shrewd eyes fixing on the Texans, then on the girl, before focussing on the befuddled and bloody captives. He put his first question to her.

"What's this all about, Mary Kate?"

She told it clearly, no rambling. As was her usual routine when in town to trade and pick up provisions, she'd had supper with friends, Selma and Bess Mooney, wife and daughter of the optimistic deputy who should have been here right now instead of probably getting lost again in the high country northwest. After supper, she had headed for Farley's Barn where her filly and the pack-mule were resting. The side alley in which her assailants had seized her was a short cut she always used. She was dragged into the old barn that should've been torn down months ago. One of the men clamped a hand about her mouth. The other tore at her clothes until she bit the man holding her and cried out for help, also scratching his face. Then these strangers, Mr Lawrence and his friend Mr Woodville, came to her aid and beat the living daylights out of her attackers.

Sheriff Dobie Hill's initial reaction caused the drifters' eyebrows to rise. He chuckled triumphantly, dropped to one knee and rolled up the right sleeve of the rogue whose face Mary Kate had clawed. More scratches, but not as fresh.

"You didn't claw his arm, just his face, right?" he growled. She frowned and nodded. "No. Milly Houseman did this last week when they jumped her in her own kitchen and broke the lamp so she couldn't identify 'em. She wasn't as lucky as you, Mary Kate. Doc Arledge's still tending her. Her nerves're shot. That time, they did what they wanted to do." He came upright, glowered at the prone men in disgust and slammed a boot to ribs pummeled by Larry a short time before. "Kelham and Gruce, damn 'em."

"Been doin' it to other women, have

they?" asked Stretch.

"For a month, I've been doing my damnedest to nail 'em," said Hill. "Trouble was I didn't know who to look for, had no leads. I started investigating after the first complaint of Peeping Toms. Milly Houseman's not the only woman they raped. There was a saloon girl too. They gave her a hell of a beating. Get comfortable, Mary Kate." He unlocked the cell-block door and gestured to the tall men. "I'd appreciate your help."

All Hill had to do was open a cell. It was small and had only one bunk. With relish of which the lawman approved, the trouble-shooters tossed Kelham and Gruce in there. He relocked the cell and led them back to his office.

"Mister Lawrence said you got to have a statement from me," Mary Kate recalled.

"Mister Lawrence knows something about the law," remarked Hill. "Affidavits, and not just from you. From him and his buddy, too." He moved to the street doorway and bellowed a name. "Clinton! Billy Clinton!" A pause, then an answer from somewhere across the street. "Need you, Billy! Get over here!" Withdrawing from the doorway, he explained to the Texans, "Billy runs a general store, happens to be a justice of the peace too. He put his John Hancock to your affidavits, I've got evidence enough for the circuit judge next time he comes to Tyson. Mightn't be for months. Those woman-beaters can sweat it out till then, after which you can bet your boots they'll be shipped to a state prison — which'll be their address for many a year to come."

"We're lookin' at a happy badge-toter," Stretch remarked, as Hill flopped into his desk chair.

"Well, he sure don't look miserable," grinned Larry.

Hill was gleeful.

"If there's one breed of scum I hate, it's the Kelhams and Gruces, the kind who want their way with women and don't give a damn how much they make a woman suffer," he declared. "I guess I hate 'em as much — or more — than I hate gunslicks who shoot a man in the back, or rustlers or horse thieves."

The tall strangers assured him they shared his disgust. He asserted all rapists should be hanged.

"That'd be fittin'," Larry agreed.

"You're a good kid, Mary Kate," said Hill. "You sure don't deserve manhandling."

She smiled amiably.

"You're a good man, Sheriff Hill," she responded. "Uncle Cosmo always says it, and I say it too."

"Smart too," said Hill. "So I don't have to convince you you're beholden to these gents."

"Little lady already thanked us," shrugged Stretch.

"I thank you," said Hill, "for being in the right place at the right time."

Hearing the JP's approaching footsteps, he took three forms of affidavit from a drawer of his desk. Pudgy Billy Clinton went to work after hearing of the capture of the rapists. Hill surrendered his chair. Clinton inked a pen and invited Mary Kate to say her piece.

"Slow and careful, Mary Kate, so I can write it all down."

He put her statement, then her rescuers' on paper, had them append their signatures, then witnessed them. For good measure, Hill also signed the affidavits. The JP said good-night and left, and the girl took that to mean she too could be on her way.

"Got to head back to the claim now," she announced, nodding and smiling at the tall men.

As she hurried away, the Texans frowned and began rising, and Hill read their minds.

"Don't worry about her," he soothed. "In daylight, moonlight or pitch dark, she knows the mountains like she knows her own face."

"But she's just a kid," Larry protested.

"You jaspers saved her from Kelham and Gruce and I give you credit for that," said Hill. "But never get the idea she's a frail and helpless kid. She's tougher than she looks and, with that rifle of hers, she doesn't often miss. Word gets around. No prospector with the women-itch messes with her. It'd be a year since one of 'em stopped her at night on her way up to old Cosmo's Double C claim. He offered to see her home safe, but she guessed what he had in mind. She discouraged him — with a bullet."

"Killed him?" frowned Stretch.

"Didn't go that far," grinned Hill. "If she'd wanted to, he'd be six feet under in the Tyson graveyard now. He's still around, but he limps nowadays. Doc Arledge says he always will."

"Shot him in a foot," guessed Larry.

"Without dismounting, and it was dark that night," nodded Hill. "Gents, any girl who can shoot that smart . . ."

"All right, so she's tough and smart and quite a sharp-shooter,"

Larry conceded. "But she's female and young."

"And you'll keep right on frettin' about her," opined his partner.

Hill offered advice. It would not be wise for them to follow her. Hearing riders to her rear, Mary Kate Feeney was apt to rein up and trigger a warning slug or three in their direction just to be sure they'd keep their distance. One of them could stop a bullet.

"If you're all that concerned, wait till morning before visiting the claim," he urged. "Come by after breakfast and I'll show you the route." He gestured to his wall-map, then said knowingly, "I guess it's only natural you'd be interested. She's a southerner — like you — and so's her Uncle Cosmo."

"We like to help folks," Stretch said casually. "Don't matter if they're from north or south."

"Well," said Hill, as they turned to leave. "If you decide to help old Cosmo and the girl work their claim, all you'll get are callouses and sore backs. No gold to be mined in this part of the Rockies. Plenty diggers, whole outfits, busting their guts up there, but few of them see any yellow."

"Might be some other help they need," said Larry. "Only way we'll find out is go visit 'em."

As they dawdled toward a saloon, Stretch urged his partner be patient.

"We couldn't bird-dog her at night anyway, and the sheriff ain't frettin' about her, says she can look out for herself. If you care all that much, there's always manana, runt. Sheriff'll tell us how to find their claim."

"Just a kid," brooded Larry.

"Sure," nodded Stretch. "But plenty smart and plenty tough."

"Girl her age, it's good she's smart," muttered Larry. "But it's bad she's got to be so hard-boiled."

"What choice does a kid like her have?" challenged Stretch. "Livin' with her uncle, helpin' him work his claim, huntin' for cash and trade goods, that's all she knows how to do."

They stopped by a saloon, downed a drink or two and decided to call it a day. If they were boneweary, they weren't about to admit it to themselves, for they believed they were as husky at this time as they'd been in their teens and twenties, the war years and the hard years since. Age slowing them down? No, they'd never admit to that.

* * *

Around 10 p.m., when the Texans wooed sleep in their two-bed room at the hotel, a marauder stealthily advanced on the Double C claim. He was lean, lethal and gold-greedy and his name was Jesse Rodd. Afoot now, having left his horse tied in the pines southeast of the hillside into which Cosmo Coote had bored his shaft, he crept through the gloom and bellied down to probe the darkness with venal eyes. He was playing a hunch that had been gnawing at him for quite a time.

From where he lay, as his eyes grew accustomed to the gloom, he stared to the rough shack, the pole corral accommodating the old man's calico gelding and, over to the left, the shafthead at the base of the rise. No light showed from the shack. Cosmo Coote, he assured himself, was deep in slumber. If the calico didn't nicker, he could make it to the shaft and do some snooping, hopefully to confirm his hunch. Flat ground now separated him from the entrance to the tunnel in which the old man and his niece had toiled so long. Grinning in anticipation, he rose.

Slowly, cautiously, he moved across the open ground to the shafthead. Three feet inside of it, the gloom was intense; he could see nothing. Take a chance, strike a match? Sure. Just long enough for a quick scan. He scratched a match to life on the butt of his holstered Colt. By its light, he noted the sides and ceiling of the shaft were well-shored. That much he saw before lighting his second match.

He took a few paces forward, gawking. To his left, sacks and pokes, old floursacks and gunnysacks were piled high — and bulging. Near the bottom of the heap, fabric had split, offering a glimpse of the contents of one sack — gleaming! The match burned down to his fingers. He dropped it, cursing. It was pitch dark again, but he was in no doubt as to what those pokes contained.

'I could tote just one of 'em out of here,' he decided.

'Then Max and the others'll have to allow I was right all along.'

He took another step toward the pile, then froze with his scalp crawling and his heart skipping a beat. The sound came from the dim rear of the shaft, low and guttural at first, then rising, filling the confined space with its echoing, gut-chilling roar. It was blood-curdling, an unearthly edge to it, a sound he had never heard before. Grizzly? Cougar? He wasn't waiting to find out. Terror unfroze his limbs. He turned and beat a frantic retreat, quitting the shaft and crossing the flat ground as fast as his feet could move.

From the shack doorway, an angry challenge followed by a rifle-shot. The slug missed Rodd by inches, and then he was charging into the timber and his challenger had not been given time to recognize him — even if he were capable of seeing in the dark.

He ran on, trembling in fear. Oh, hell! Old Coote had to be loco, that brat girl too! What kind of varmint did they keep chained in that shaft? Must be chained, otherwise it would have jumped him and he wouldn't be running now. The roar could only come from an animal of great size, big enough to bring him down and tear him apart. He was sweating by the time he reached his horse, untied it and swung astride.

The old man in the shack doorway lowered his rifle. Clouds cleared the moon and its pallid glow now lit the area. He swore bitterly, then grinned, heaved a sigh of relief and called softly, "Good boy, Rufe. Did your duty."

The animal that had struck mortal fear into the marauder strutted out of the shaft and came to him to have his head patted and his floppy ears fondled. No mastiff this dog. Twenty-four inches at most from tip of nose to curve of rump, a small dog of chunky build and shaggy reddish-brown pelt. Handsome never. Ugly was the word for this little beast of questionable pedigree found as a whimpering pup by Mary Kate Feeney two years before.

Cosmo Coote patted and fondled. Rufe licked a gnarled hand and wagged his thick-furred tail. His bark was gruff and, depending on the identity of the human barked at, challenging or joyful. His growl was something else. It was the growl that had terrified the marauder, always seeming to start from his belly. Rising in volume, echoing along the shaft, it had all the loud and ferocious quality of an enraged grizzly or mountain lion.

"Now you get on back and rest some more," urged Cosmo, rising to withdraw into the shack. He was no taller than his niece, well on in years, his thatch and whiskers ash-grey. But he was durable and still active, carrying no excess fat, muscles still hard. "I'm gonna stoke the stove and heat up the coffee. She'll be back from town pretty soon."

Rufe obeyed. Cosmo lit the lamp in the poky kitchen and set about heating coffee. The other room was longer and his and his niece's sleeping quarters weren't divided by a wall; patched and aged blankets hanging from rope secured to front and rear walls guaranteed Mary Kate's maidenly privacy while dressing or sleeping.

Some forty-five minutes later, he heard the familiar hoofbeats, his niece's black filly and the pack-mule, then Rufe's barked greeting and her affectionate response. She offsaddled her filly, corraled both animals and joined her uncle with the dog at her heels.

"Got everything, huh?" he remarked, watching her stash the provisions.

"Did real good," she bragged. "Our regulars dealt square just like always."

"Your duds're torn," he frowned.

"You set, I'll pour the coffee and tell you all about it," she offered.

They sat at the rough table and, while sipping coffee, she recounted her experience in Tyson and its aftermath, the violent apprehension of lecherous Kelham and his crony. Having heard it all, Cosmo scowled indignantly.

"Trash." He snarled the word.

"Best forgotten, Uncle Cosmo," she shrugged. She finished her coffee. Rufe promptly scrambled onto her lap. "They'll get punishment aplenty, that's for sure. And I bet, when the circuit judge shows up and holds court in Bowley's Saloon, they'll still be hurtin' from what them tall fellers did to 'em."

"Helluva thing," growled Cosmo.

"I clawed and bit — I thought I was riled," she recalled. "But, oh glory, if you could've seen how them tall fellers tore into 'em! I declare they punch like they got rocks in their fists, and they're so all-fired *strong*!"

Cosmo eyed her pensively.

"Uncommon tall?"

"One of 'em'd have to be six and a half feet, the rangy one," she declared. "And his partner ain't much shorter and he's got shoulders out to here."

She spread her arms. He nodded and asked.

"You get their names?"

"Sure, Lawrence and Woodville," she replied.

"Is that so?" he mused.

"That's so," she said. "Why?"

"You — uh — happen to notice if the taller one packs a brace of six-guns?" he prodded. "And the other feller just one?"

"Yeah, I noticed," she said.

"They'd be southerners like us." This was a statement, not a question.

"Right," she grinned. "Texans."

"I know of 'em," he said. "They only told you half of their names. Child, I've read many a newspaper, so I can say it for sure. You got yourself rescued by a couple rough wanderers with a big reputation, Larry Valentine and Stretch Emerson. Trouble-shooters is what they are, and they've been fightin' outlaws for more years than you've had birthdays."

"Famous, huh?" she asked eagerly.

"And then some," he said. "I can't guess if you'll ever see 'em again. If you do, you mind what I'm tellin' you. You can trust 'em. They're bad trouble, but only for law-breakers. Honest folks got nothin' to fear from Valentine and his buddy."

"Well, maybe I'm gettin' smarter at sizin' people up," she decided, "on account of I took to 'em right off, felt safe with 'em."

"Best we bunk down now," he said. "Tomorrow I head for Cooper City to set up some business with an old friend from way back. Figure to make an early start."

"Breakfast'll be ready when you are," she assured him. "And grub enough for you to eat regular all the way east." The eager grin flashed again. "Tomorrow's the big day, huh?"

"Mighty important day for us, child," he declared. "We're all through here. No more diggin' for us."

"No more blisters," she enthused. "No more spittin' dust and grit."

As he rose, he studied her soberly.

"It won't feel good, me ridin' east, you stayin' on to guard what's ours," he fretted. "We kept our secret good, but you're gonna have to be extra careful. Keep your rifle loaded and close enough for you to grab even when you bed down, and make sure Rufe does his sleepin' in the shaft."

"That's what we always do," she shrugged. "We've been plenty careful. Nobody knows . . . "

"Somebody just *might* know," he countered. "Little while ago, that critter spooked a snooper and woke me. I took a shot at a runnin' man, Mary Kate. Maybe scored on him, but I won't bet on it. The thing is — he was runnin' from the shaft, so there's a chance he saw our cache."

"Ain't likely," she argued. "Rufe sleeps light. He'd've fazed the snooper as he sniffed him."

"We'd better hope that's how it was," muttered Cosmo. "But . . . "

"I know," she nodded. "Don't you fret none, Uncle Cosmo. I'm keen-sighted and I can hear a snooper a long ways off. Me and Rufe'll guard the place good till you get back."

"Wish it didn't have to be this way," he sighed, stifling a yawn. "But that's how it goes. There's only you and me and that hound-dog. We're all we got in the world."

"Not all," she retorted, winking and gesturing. "We got what we mined."

"*Keepin'* it, that's what's important," he stressed. "I won't feel easy of mind till it's safe in the vault of that big bank in Cooper City, the Miners National."

"You're goin' to the right man," she said encouragingly. "Mister Stuckey won't fail you."

"Strachey — Ed Strachey," he corrected. "Ain't polite to forget a good friend's name or how to say it."

"I'll remember," she promised. "Happy dreams, Uncle Cosmo."

It was nearing midnight when Jesse Rodd returned to the claim at which he and seven others had vainly toiled this past half-year. A painted signboard on the facade of the larger of the clapboard and tarpaper cabins proclaimed this to be the Ortner Mining Company. But that title and the shafts bored into the east and west walls of the gulch were a bad joke; the pickings had been lean, negligible in fact.

Lamps still burned. Some of his cohorts, including Max Ortner himself, had not turned in and now emerged. They wore sidearms, would have felt naked without them. Prospectors? Only for the past six months. Before fleeing Southwest Nebraska after their last coup, they had robbed banks, held up stagecoaches and sent more than one honest citizen to his grave. The last pursuing posse had numbered two dozen; the gang had fled into Colorado less than a hundred yards ahead of the law.

Ortner, tall, muscular and alert-eyed, growled his challenge while Rodd was turning his mount into the corral.

"Just where the hell've you been?"

"And what spooked you?" demanded his chief henchman, long-haired Clay Merrill. "Damn it, Jesse, you're shakin' and sweatin' like you got a fever."

One of the other men, the bow-legged, pasty-faced Ritchie Boneen, chuckled jeeringly and asked, "Whatsa-matter, Jesse? Seen a ghost?"

"Didn't see what scared me, only heard it, and I don't never want to hear it again," muttered Rodd. "Max, I was right. I scouted old Coote's claim and I got plenty to tell you."

Ortner studied him a long moment, then snapped his fingers.

"Rouse the others, Ritchie. Better we all crowd into my cabin to hear this."

2

First Clash

THE other four hard cases, Joe Darrow, Leon Kaye, Zeke Pitch and Boyd Trenkler, were every inch as larcenous, as homicidal, as their cohorts. Crammed into their leader's quarters, they eyed Rodd expectantly.

"All right now," Ortner nodded to him. "On your own time and against my orders, you sneaked away to spy on the old man's claim. Always were curious about Coote, weren't you?"

"Him and the girl been workin' that lonesome claim a good long time — we all know that," said Rodd. "Why'd they stay at it so long? I said they must've made a strike, and now I've proved it!"

"We're listening," said Ortner. "Tell us what you found."

Rodd told it in faltering sentences; he was still suffering shock. Wondering glances were exchanged, but nobody interjected until he was through talking. First to comment, thick-whiskered Zeke Pitch waxed sceptical.

"No man can tame and train a grizzly, use it for guardin' a mine tunnel."

"Nor a mountain cat," insisted swarthy Leon Kaye.

"I swear it wasn't human," shuddered Rodd. "And, when it hollered at me . . . !"

"You didn't get a look at it?" prodded Ortner. Rodd shook his head. "But you did see a cache, a whole heap of full sacks and what was in one of them — no mistake about that?"

"Only raw nuggets, the pure stuff, could shine like that, Max," Rodd said vehemently.

"So it all adds up to just one possibility," mused Ortner. "And it raises a question. Have Coote and the girl mined it all, or are they still digging?"

"I didn't have much time, but the Double C shaft ain't the first worked-out claim I've seen," said Rodd. "They shored up the farther they bored and the only dirt walls I spotted had all them creases — that used to be pay-veins. I'm matchin' that to the pile of sacks and bettin' my boots they mined it all. Hell, Max, it's a bonanza!"

"And it'd be wasted on a burnt-out old packrat and a fool girl," growled hefty Boyd Trenkler, licking his thick lips.

"Divided eight ways, it'd make each of us richer than he ever hoped to be," agreed Ortner. "But grabbing it for ourselves calls for careful planning. Gold — in quantity — is quite a weight. I have to anticipate Coote's next move, stay one jump ahead of him."

"He has to ship it out some way," opined Merrill. "It don't buy him anything where it is now, stashed in his shaft. Would he load it on a mule a little at a time and take it to Tyson? Not likely, Max. There's an assay office in Tyson, but only one bank, and it's a tin can. The safe's only so big."

He held a hand three feet above the floor. The other men grunted agreement.

"A bigger town," decided Ortner. "If not Denver, north to Melgosa or east to Cooper City, towns with bigger banks. A shipment that size would be consigned to a bank with a vault. No safe could hold it. A strongroom, yes, not just a safe. So that means Denver, Melgosa or Cooper City. Then there's the important question of transportation. Coote has to arrange that, and I doubt he'd hire rigs or a whole herd of pack-mules by mail. He'll be wary about anything on paper." He won sardonic laughter with his next comment. "Stagecoaches are sometimes ambushed and mailsacks hijacked."

They were his to command, Merrill

included. Before his greed and anti-social instincts led him into crime, Max Ortner had completed his education. He was confident, cunning and contemptuous of the law-abiding, and the seven hard cases were in awe of him. Until Jesse Rodd embarked on his spying expedition to the Double C claim, none had defied his orders. But he would not reprimand Rodd, now that the scrawny gunman had broken the secret of the Coote cache.

"Could happen any time now you think?" prodded Merrill. "The old man or the girl're gonna head for one of them big towns?"

"Any time now," nodded Ortner. "So, before daylight, I want one of you watching Double C." He chose Darrow. "You first. Take my telescope, get a high vantage-point and just watch and wait. Four-hour watches. We'll all take our turn. When they make their move, the watcher will get back here fast. That's all we need to know, the direction he or she is travelling."

"For starters," guessed Trenkler.

"Yes, for starters," said Ortner. "After that, more watching and waiting. I can't plan an ambush until I know where they're shipping the gold and by what means."

"Yeah, okay," grinned Darrow. "By sun-up, I'll be keepin' my eyes peeled. Up a tree maybe or atop a rockmound. Whoever's gonna take over from me, he only has to follow my tracks."

"One other thing, Max," Merrill said before they filed out of Ortner's cabin. "We're short on fresh meat. Somebody better hunt us some chow."

"You," said Ortner, nodding to Kaye. "And, this time, try stalking deer for a change or bring down a few quail. I'm tired of eating jackrabbit stew."

"Do my best," Kaye shrugged. "But I can only shoot what I can flush out!"

* * *

By 8.30 of the following morning, while the Texans were studying the map in the sheriff's office and listening to Dobie Hill's directions, Cosmo Coote was mounting his calico to begin his journey.

The old man had dressed for the occasion. His black 'going to meeting' suit still fitted. Over it he wore a duster, and his headgear was a felt hat not as decrepit as the tile worn during long and arduous toil in the heat and dust of the mine tunnel.

"Ride safe," Mary Kate urged, as she secured a sack of provisions to his saddle. "This'll be good for you, Uncle Cosmo, visitin' an old friend again."

"Been a long time," Cosmo said wistfully. "Ed did just fine for himself, built up his own business, got a wife and young'uns."

She clambered up to kiss him, lowered herself without treading on Rufe, always at her feet, and reminded him, "You got your own young'un — me — even if you're still a bachelor-man."

"That's so," he nodded. "All right

now, best be on my way. It's a fair piece from here to Cooper City. Don't you forget nothin' I told you. I'm leavin' our fortune with you and countin' on you to tend it good. You got plenty grub, so you stay put till I get back, hear?"

"Don't you be frettin'," she grinned. "And forget about that snooper. Any fool shows his face around here, I'll plumb shoot his hat off and, if that don't send him runnin', I'll drop my sights and put a bullet through his head. We toiled too hard to lose what's ours, right?"

"Right," he said.

Rufe accorded him a farewell bark as he turned the calico and started eastward, a move that would soon be reported to Max Ortner.

The Texans had no difficulty following Mary Kate's sign up the winding mountain trail, her filly and the mule having left clear tracks. They were in no hurry, just wanted to assure themselves the girl had reached her destination without mishap.

At ease, smoking, they let their horses take the grades, some steep, some gentle, at their own pace. Then, when they were on eighty yards of level trail some distance west of the Ortner mine, their relaxed mood was shattered by the bark of a Winchester and the nerve-jolting sensation of a .44.40 slug passing close enough for them to feel its wind on their faces. They cursed, dropped hands to holsters and, as a jeering laugh reached them from somewhere to their right, drew rein.

Larry flicked his half-smoked quirley away and soothed his startled sorrel. Stretch did the same for his pinto. And then they turned in their saddles to stare at the laughing man, a swarthy, roughly-garbed hombre squatting cross-legged atop a low rise.

Leon Kaye had a perverted sense of humor.

"Well, pardon me all to hell," he called; it didn't sound like an apology. "Out huntin'. Mistook you jaspers for a couple jackrabbits."

"The hell he did," Stretch said softly.

"He's mine," Larry said just as softly.

"Make the sonofagun regret," urged Stretch.

"Count on it," said Larry.

"Man, oh man!" guffawed Kaye. "If you could've seen the look on your kissers. Scared hell outa you, huh?"

Slowly, Larry dismounted and passed his rein to his sidekick. He moved off the trail and began climbing the near slope of the rise and, from atop it, Kaye read no expression on his face and went right on laughing. Not till Larry climbed closer did he note the steely glint in his eyes. He began rising and made to lever a fresh shell into his rifle's breach, but by then, it was too late.

Reaching him, Larry got his left hand to the Winchester's barrel. He wrenched it from Kaye's grasp, bunched his right and threw a short jab — short but powerful. Blood spurting from his damaged nose, Kaye grunted in pain and flopped on his backside. Next, Larry took a fistful of his shirtfront, lifted him upright and backhanded him twice.

"It was — just a joke!" gasped Kaye.

"That so?" challenged Larry. "So pardon me if you're hurtin'. I'm a joker too, just foolin' around."

He whisked the swarthy man's colt from its holster, transferred it to his own waistband and beckoned Stretch, who unhurriedly put his mount to the slope, leading the sorrel by its rein.

"What's the matter with you two?" Kaye tried blustering. "Can't you take a joke?"

Stretch arrived, frowned at him and said grimly, "A joke?"

"That's what he says," nodded Larry. "You laughin?"

"Not so you'd notice," growled Stretch.

"Who are you and where're you from?" demanded Larry.

"Leon Kaye," mumbled the swarthy man, dabbing at his aching nose with a bandana. "From the Ortner minin' outfit."

"So listen good, Leon Kaye from the Ortner minin' outfit," scowled Larry. "Fun is fun, but only a fool pulls such a dumb trick. We felt the wind of the slug, and we don't much appreciate that feelin'."

"I'm a sure shot," protested Kaye. "Aimed to miss you."

"*You* claim you're a sure shot," retorted Stretch. "All me and my partner're thinkin' of right now is how dead we'd be — one of us anyway — if that damn bullet'd come an inch closer."

Spotting Kaye's tied horse, Larry picked up the fallen rifle and fetched the animal.

"Fill your saddle — joker," he ordered. "We're takin' you back where you came from. I got a thing or two to say to your boss."

"Listen, that wouldn't be the smartest

idea you ever had, big man," warned Kaye, but he mounted the horse. "I work with a tough bunch. My buddies won't take kindly to this. You're buyin' yourself more trouble than you can handle."

"Funny you should say that," Larry coldly countered. "The way we feel right now, we'll welcome any trouble your buddies want to start."

"Let's go," said Stretch. "And don't try drawin' us away from where you toil, funny man. We'll be backtrackin' your critter."

A while later, hearing approching horses, Ortner's men did what was expected of them, reacting as they had reacted on the few other occasions riders had stopped by. Darrow and Boneen hustled into one shaft to swing pickaxes, Merrill, Pitch and Rodd into the other, while Ortner emerged from his cabin with his thumbs hooked in the armholes of his vest; Boyd Trenkler was taking his turn at keeping the Coote claim under observation.

When their crony and his captors stalled their mounts in front of Ortner, the hard cases quit the shafts, noted Kaye's condition and warily appraised the tall men.

"You the boss here?" Larry growled at Ortner.

"Max Ortner — and do you mind explaining this?" was the cool response.

"That's what we're here for," drawled Stretch.

Larry tugged Kaye's pistol from his Levis and tossed it and the rifle to the dust.

"You can get down," he told Kaye curtly, but with his eyes on Ortner. As the swarthy man dismounted, he said his piece. "This bonehead took a shot at us. A joke he claims, but we didn't take it as no joke because the bullet came a helluva lot too close for comfort."

"So you spooked and got mad and beat up on Leon," accused Darrow. "Two against one. Real brave heroes you are."

"Be quiet," Ortner chided him. "I'll handle this."

"Damn right you will," declared Larry. "That's what bein' a boss means, Ortner. You hire men, you have to keep 'em in line, make sure they use the brains they were born with and don't do nothin' stupid."

"Now, see here . . ." began Ortner.

"I ain't through talkin'," said Larry.

"So it would seem," Ortner said dryly.

"Be thankful we didn't deliver that jackass dead, hung over his horse," said Larry. "Mostly, when some trigger-happy no-account takes a shot at us, we fill our hands fast and shoot back."

"He don't savvy how lucky he is," said Stretch. "He laughed right after he triggered at us — so we guessed he just wasn't real bright, likely a mite tetched."

"Am I makin' it clear for you, Ortner?" asked Larry. "From here on, do what a boss ought to do. Keep Kaye and your other hands workin'. That'll be healthier for 'em because, if any of 'em act as foolish as Kaye, it could be the death of 'em."

"I'm sure Leon meant no harm," said Ortner. "And now, if you're through being unreasonable and abusive, you'd best leave. You're on my land, so technically you're trespassing."

Now the trouble-shooters shifted their gaze to match stares with the fuming Kaye and the other men.

"How about this, amigo?" grinned Stretch. "Trespassin' we are. Why, we ought to be plumb ashamed."

"Any of you heroes want to do somethin' about it?" challenged Larry.

"Listen, you . . . !" scowled Merrill.

"Forget it, Clay," ordered Ortner.

"Good advice," said Larry.

And, with that, he and his partner departed, but cautiously and in a way that proved no Ortner man could fill his hand without their knowing it. At that, it was quite a feat of horsemanship. The sorrel and pinto were well-trained to their riders' needs and commands.

They backed away from the claim so that, while ever they were still in sight of Ortner's crew, the Texans had *them* in clear view. They guided their mounts with their knees, reins held in left hands, right hands on gunbutts.

Ortner didn't speak until the tall horsemen had disappeared.

"Fool move," he reprimanded Kaye. "Do nothing so rash again, understand? This set-up is our front. We're supposed to be working a mine, not drawing attention to ourselves by fazing riders using the mountain trail."

"Those bastards!" gasped Kaye.

"Smart-alecks," sneered Boneen.

"Everybody simmer down," muttered Merrill. "Max is right. He's always right. That's why we follow his orders, why he's the boss. At a time like this, playin' for high stakes, we oughtn't be tanglin' with strangers."

"Pick up your weapons and go hunt us some fresh meat," Ortner commanded Kaye. He gestured brusquely. "In that direction. Stay far clear of the trail — in case you're tempted to make a fool of yourself again."

Back on the trail, pushing onward and upward, the Texans traded opinions about Max Ortner and his men.

"At runnin' a mine, he's a greenhorn," Stretch said scathingly. "Plain enough he's got education but, when it comes to bossin' a hard case crew, he's plenty dumb."

"Might be his hired hands got plenty to learn too," mused Larry. "You notice they were heeled?"

"Uh huh," grunted Stretch. "Every one of 'em."

"They never worked in no other mine tunnels, or maybe they're just plain careless," decided Larry.

"Hey now." Stretch eyed him side-long. "I didn't think . . . "

"You're no lamebrain," shrugged Larry. "You'd've thought of it soon enough."

"Last time we helped work a shaft, we had to draw up our bandanas to keep the dust out — and we left our hardware outside," Stretch recalled. "That dust, helluva lot of it . . . "

"Gets into everything," nodded Larry. "Your hair, your ears. It's in the air, with you all the time."

"And it'd sure get into a man's holster and the innards of what's in the holster," frowned Stretch. "A smart hombre'd just never work in all that dirt with his hardware strapped on. Hell, you wouldn't keep a rifle, any kind of weapon, in a mine tunnel. Next time you had to use it, it'd be full of grit, could backfire." Having figured this out, he added, "You know, they looked more like gunslingers than minehands."

"Ornery bunch," agreed Larry. "And Ortner himself. I don't know how far I'd trust him. No farther'n I could see him, I guess."

It was getting toward noon when they sighted and approached the Double C claim. Smoke rose lazily from the shack's kitchen chimney. They recognized the filly and the mule in the corral. No sign of the girl. Inside the shack, they supposed, hadn't heard them. But something else had.

They reined up, but not to dismount. Larry's sorrel was balking, nickering shrilly and fighting his efforts at bringing it under control. The Texans traded shocked and wondering stares, for the ominous inhuman growl echoing from the shaft defied definition. In their years of wandering, animals of every kind had challenged them, cougars, bears, enraged bulls — but what kind of creature was this?

"Hell, runt . . ." breathed Stretch.

"Don't ask me," Larry said tensely. "You think *I* ever heard such a critter?"

Mary Kate didn't ease their shock by emerging from the shack and happily waving to them. Was she deaf? To them, it was an unnatural, incomprehensible situation, she seemingly oblivious to that persistent unearthly cry, smiling so cheerfully. But then, mercifully, she noted their startled expressions, cupped her hands about her mouth and yelled toward the shaft.

"Hush up, Rufe! *Friendlies!*" The roaring promptly ceased. She showed her visitors a reassuring grin. "No need to fret. He only comes bitin' and clawin' when I holler 'hostiles', understands them two words good."

Rufe now ambled out of the shaft, wagging his tail and showing his tongue, but not his teeth. He surveyed the horsemen with no hint of suspicion, while they gaped at him. The sorrel and the pinto at once relaxed; it took their owners a little longer.

"It was the dog did all that hell-roarin'?" Larry challenged incredulously.

"Just Rufe," nodded Mary Kate. "Come to think of it, I never ever heard any other dog growl exactly like he does. And, when he's inside the mine, it sounds like . . ."

"Sounds powerful loud." Stretch's voice shook. "And it ain't natural. Why, it's like you got a critter double the size of a grizzly in there."

"That's handy," offered Mary Kate. "For scarin' off snoopers, you know?"

"Well, yeah," sighed Larry. "If that noise don't spook 'em, they'd have to be uncommon brave."

Rufe came closer, sniffed at the sorrel's left forehoof, then cocked a hind leg and relieved himself against it. Larry's mount's reaction was eloquent. He lowered his head to study the small hound and, if horses could speak, would surely have declared, 'For a mutt your size, you got a lot of nerve.'

"Too bad Uncle Cosmo ain't here," said the girl. "He'd've been right glad to meet you. Seems he knows all about you."

"He does?" prodded Stretch.

"Why, sure," she said. "You're Larry and Stretch, he said. And a girl can trust you." She invited them to cool their saddles and corral their animals. "Stay and eat, huh? All I gotta do is throw some more beans and taters in the pot."

"You're all alone here?" asked Larry.

"Nope," she grinned. "Got Rufe for company — and protection. And, if trouble-makers don't run when he hollers, I got my rifle."

The tall men dismounted, led their horses to the corral and saw to their comfort. Rufe was sticking close. Had they really won his approval? He proved they had when they hunkered, came close, sniffed at them and licked their hands. Stretch stroked his head. The dog didn't flinch, so plainly he savvied the word 'friendlies'.

Lounging in the shack doorway, watching Mary Kate busying herself at the stove, they kept the conversation going.

"Don't seem right," remarked Larry. "I'll allow you take care of yourself good, Mary Kate, but you and your Uncle got a lonesome claim here."

"Long ways from anywhere," said Stretch.

"Got everything we need," she shrugged. "Water's good. You likely noticed the little spring back of the shack a fair piece from the privy."

"But just you and Rufe," argued Larry.

"It was that time," she calmly explained. "Uncle Cosmo couldn't hold back from it no longer. Some things can't wait, you know? So he headed east right after breakfast."

"Where's he bound?" asked Stretch. "He travellin' far?"

"All the way east to Cooper City," she said. "Got a good friend there. Ed Strachey bosses a freight outfit, a big'un. They were in the war together. Well, same regiment. Ed Strachey was an officer, Uncle Cosmo just a foot soldier."

"Infantry outfit," mused Stretch.

"Uh huh," she nodded. "Confederate army, just like you and Larry." She turned to give them a shrewd once-over. "You — uh — all that worried about me, thinkin' of hangin' round till Uncle Cosmo comes back?"

"Mary Kate, you're good with a rifle and Rufe's plumb loyal," frowned

Larry. "But you're still just a kid and a dog, and there's mean hombres in this high country. We had a run-in with a bunch of 'em on our way here."

"You see, honey, we got nothin' better to do," said the taller Texan. "So, if you ain't objectin' . . . "

"We'll help Rufe guard this place," said Larry. "That okay?"

"Fine by me," she enthused. "After we eat, I'll explain you why Uncle Cosmo's headed for Cooper City. He wouldn't mind me tellin' you. Said you ain't thieves and it's only outlaw trash you make a trouble for."

It was a rough but nourishing lunch. While the girl badgered her guests with questions about their eventful career, Rufe accounted for his portion, took a drink of water from his bowl in a corner, then curled up in the open doorway, not for an after lunch nap, but to let his eyes wander warily over the surrounding terrain. Vigilance, it seemed, was the scruffy mongrel's dominant instinct.

Mary Kate's coffee was passable. After refills, the guests built and lit their after-lunch cigarettes and eyed her patiently. They didn't need to let their pants-belts out a notch; somehow, for whatever reason, they had stayed flat-bellied through the years, building muscle maybe, but no excess fat. Studying Mary Kate, Larry was secretly wistful. She was feminine enough, despite his never having seen her in female attire. The face and figure were softly contoured but, with her shirt-sleeves rolled high, the arms showed muscle. The hands were well-shaped, but calloused; this cheerful, likable girl was more than casually acquainted with physical labor, a lot of it.

"Sheriff told us you've been helpin' your uncle ever since he staked out this claim," he recalled.

"Well, sure," she nodded. "He took care of me after my folks died. I was only little then. But, when I started growin', I sure wasn't gonna be no burden to him, just naturally shared chores. I can swing an ax good as any man. All the timber it took to shore up our shaft, I helped cut it. Just as handy with a pickax too, worked right along with Uncle Cosmo."

When their cigarettes were smoked down, she decided now was as good a time as any for dealing them in on her and her uncle's secret. They would be the first, she reflected as she led them to the shaft. But her uncle would approve. If he trusted them on the strength of all he'd read and heard of them, why shouldn't she?

At her command, Rufe sat guard at the entrance. The Texans moved in after her and waited while she reached to a small ledge holding a lamp and a tin of wax vestas. She lit the lamp and most of the tunnel could now be studied, the dirt floor, the stoutly shored walls and ceiling — and the formidable mound of filled sacks. The material varied. The tall men saw gunnysacks, pokes fashioned of animal hide, floursacks, all secured by knotted rawhide strips.

"That's all of it," Mary Kate said calmly. "Took us a lot of years. See the dug-out veins? We didn't quit till there was no more yellow to be gouged out of here." She bent from the hips and squinted. "Consarn. One of 'em split. I'll have to do some stitchin' there."

"Are you tellin' us . . . ?" began Larry.

"Take a look for yourself," she urged.

"Whatsamatter, runt?" Stretch frowned at his partner.

"*You* take a look," muttered Larry. "All of a sudden, my feet feel like they're stuck to ground."

Stretch shrugged, lifted a poke from atop the pile, remarked on its weight, then hunkered to unknot the rawhide tie. He shoved his fingers in, loosed a gasp, then exhibited the four gleaming nuggets on his palm; his hand shook. "Holy Hannah!"

Larry sighed heavily. They were

seeing the stuff of which dreams are made, the precious metal for which some men toiled, some men bartered and many men killed. How could the girl be so serene? Why wasn't she trembling? He must have voiced this thought, because she said offhandedly.

"I'm used to it. Helped mine it and bag it and pile it."

She relieved bug-eyed Stretch of the small chore of returning the nuggets to the poke and resecuring it; she didn't think him capable, and neither did Larry.

"You got — a fortune here," he said huskily.

"Enough to last Uncle Cosmo and me the rest of our lives," she agreed. "No more diggin' and sweatin'. Livin' easy we'll be. Listen, if you're gonna help guard it . . ."

"Well — uh huh — we better do that," mumbled Stretch.

"Might's well help yourselves," she offered. "Stash some in your saddlebag.

Uncle Cosmo'd want to pay for your help."

"That ain't our way," said Larry. "Sometimes we take pay for what we do, but most time we don't, and this'll be one of those times."

He discovered he had regained the power of locomotion, was able to trudge out of the shaft. Mary Kate killed the lamp and followed him with Stretch at her heels. Outside, he produced his hip-wallet and invited her inspection of its contents.

"Like you can see, honey, we got all the dinero we need — and more," said Stretch.

"We gamble some," said Larry. "And, once in a while, we'll let some rich jasper pay us for helpin' him out. Now, Mary Kate, you and Uncle Cosmo ain't gonna owe us none of your gold. What we aim to do won't cost you a dime, but it's for sure we're gonna do it."

"I should hope," Stretch said vehemently.

"I've guessed why your uncle's makin' a deal with his old compadre that runs a freight line," Larry told the girl. "That heap'll weigh heavy. To ship it — well — that'll be work for freight wagons and strong teams. He didn't have no choice but to go parley with Strachey personal, so he had to leave you here, just you and Rufe to guard your fortune. Maybe you'd manage fine, no trouble, 'tween now and when the freighters get here, but my partner and me want to be sure so, if you got no objection, here's where we stay till we ain't needed no more."

"Hey, that'll be fine!" she grinned. "One of you can sleep in Uncle Cosmo's bunk and . . . !"

"Honey, we won't be bunkin' in Uncle Cosmo's room," said Larry. "And we won't both be sleepin' at the same time. Now that Rufe knows we're friendlies, he won't mind if one of us beds down in the shaft."

"*One* of us," Stretch emphasized.

"We'll be guardin' your piece of this high country, one of us patrollin' while one of us sleeps."

"Sounds good," she agreed. "Only I'll take my turn. I can sit guard while both of you get some sleep."

"Well, maybe," said Larry. "We'll see. Meanwhile, how're you fixed for firewood?"

"Got plenty," she said. "Plenty for cookin' for three 'stead of just me and Rufe." She eyed the dog affectionately. "And, listen, whichever of you's sittin' guard, it won't matter if you get drowsy and start dozin'. Won't be no snooper could reach you before Rufe caught his scent. That's what happened last night before I got back from town."

The Texans traded glances.

"*What* happened last night?" demanded Larry.

"Rufe sniffed a prowler, growled up a storm and scared him good, roused Uncle Cosmo."

"And?"

"Uncle Cosmo didn't get a clear

look at him, took a shot at him just the same. I don't reckon *that* jasper'd be brave enough to try sneakin' back again."

Larry thoughtfully tugged at an ear. Stretch gazed around casually and remarked, "I could use some exercise, and extra firewood's always handy."

"Sure," nodded Larry. "And somethin' in my saddlebag might help."

"Just what I was thinkin'," nodded Stretch.

He went to where he and his partner had dumped their gear, took the field-glasses from Larry's saddlebag and trudged away.

It was after 2 p.m. when he returned to the site of the Double C claim hefting as much wood as he could tote, the field-glasses dangling by their strap from his shoulder. Larry was in the corral, treating the sorrel and pinto to a rubdown, Mary Kate perched on the rail trading talk with him, the dog catnapping on sun-warmed ground nearby.

In response to his question, the girl dropped from the rail.

"I'll show you where to stash it," she offered. "Then I better get to cuttin' meat and peelin' taters. We'll have us a fine supper tonight, beef stew that'll melt in your mouth."

After Stretch had dumped the wood and Mary Kate was getting busy in her kitchen, he returned the field-glasses to Larry's saddlebag, propped a shoulder against a corral post and fished out his makings. Larry postponed his chores to move close to him.

"Cut his sign?" he asked quietly.

"Uh huh," grunted Stretch. "One man. He made off through the trees over thataway. I don't reckon Cosmo scored on him."

"Found the bullet?"

"Dug it out of a tree. The snooper kept right on runnin'. I found where he left his horse. No more bootprints then. Just hoofprints. I tagged 'em a ways. Well, far enough to get a notion whichaway he was headed."

"So?"

"Can't stake my life, runt, but it might be he rid to the Ortner mine."

Larry grimaced, scratched a match and held it to his partner's quirley.

"Somethin' to think about, huh?" drawled Stretch. "Supposin' now he spotted the stash before Rufe spooked him . . ."

"Yeah." Larry nodded grimly. "Somethin' to think about."

The new guardians of Double C were maintaining vigilance when, several days later, Cosmo Coote reached his destination.

3

Camouflage

THE old man hadn't seen a town so big, so bustling, in a long time, but was not at all self-conscious; nothing like mining a fortune to give a man confidence. Pride too, come to think of it.

He idled his mount past the impressive office of the Strachey Freight Line en route to a livery stable and grinned approvingly. To each his own. His old friend had established a business and tasted success long before his pickax had revealed part of a pay-vein; he had dug only two feet into the hillside at that time.

After stabling his horse, he ambled back to the Strachey headquarters, but did not at once enter the front office. He moved around back to the wide yard accommodating sizeable vehicles and corraled team-animals and subjected those animals to a keen appraisal. Just right for hauling heavy cargoes, he observed. Big, broad-backed, strong-limbed. And the wagons? Strong enough too. Wouldn't they have born heavy loads, farm equipment, anvils, consignments of the merchandise stocked by hardware merchants of towns not served by the railroads? And freighters didn't just drive wagons. They had to be versatile, able to effect running repairs to harness, re-shoe a horse, replace a wheel, fix damaged axles.

He returned to Main Street and entered the office. Behind the counter, a thin man wearing an eyeshade and sleeve-protectors was making entries in a ledger. A door in the rear wall was closed and proclaimed the room beyond, in neat lettering, to be the private office of E. J. Strachey, Proprietor. He moved to the counter. The book-keeper looked up and nodded.

"'Morning. Help you?"

Cosmo nodded to the connecting door.

"Anybody with your boss right now?"

"No, not right now."

"Here to parley with him. We know each other from way back."

"Fine, I'll tell him you're here. Can I ask the name?"

"Cosmo Coote."

"Certainly, Mister Coote. Care to take a seat?"

Cosmo grinned gently.

"Waste of time, son. Before I could get my butt onto a chair, you'd be takin' me in there."

"I believe you," said the bookkeeper, flashing him an answering grin.

He hurried to the other door, knocked and entered, and Cosmo cocked an ear. There was an immediate response from a familiar voice.

"Show him in, Vern! Show him in rightaway!"

The bookkeeper reappeared, nodding,

holding the door wide. He closed it again after Cosmo crossed the threshold. Strachey, well-groomed, burly and blunt-featured, stood behind a paper-littered desk grinning broadly and offering his hand.

"Howdy," greeted Cosmo. "You look like — uh — the lady you hitched up with feeds you good."

"Cosmo, you sawn-off old fossicker, put it there!" beamed Strachey. "Great to see you!"

The warm handshake wasn't enough for the hefty freight-boss; he came around his desk to wrap his arms about the little man, lift him off his feet and deposit him in a chair. Cosmo grinned indulgently. Strachey reseated himself and, for a long moment, they matched stares.

"Been a long time," Cosmo said wistfully.

"Writing to each other was good, but this is better," grinned Strachey. "You're looking fine. I'd guess you've worked long and hard since I last saw you, but hard work must agree with you."

"Worth it," said Cosmo. "You done good too. Biggest freight outfit in the state, huh?"

"Well, North Colorado anyway," said Strachey.

They had one thing in common, a bond so strong that the contrast in their backgrounds — Cosmo was Mississippi-born and of humble origins, Strachey a Virginian of good family and superior education — seemed of little significance, if any.

"Business boomin' for you?" asked Cosmo.

"Never better, but big problems right now," complained Strachey. "If you've just arrived, you mightn't have heard about it yet. An influenza epidemic here. A third of the Cooper City population came down with it. The worst is over according to local doctors. One of my kids fell victim to it, but is recovering now. My problem is, for some reason I'll never understand, half of my drivers and loaders were stricken. No fatalities. They're at the recovery stage, but still not fit for duty, so the Strachey line is short-staffed at the moment. It'll be another week before my crews are back to full strength."

Cosmo frowned worriedly.

"That ain't good, Ed. Seems I'm needin' your help at a bad time."

"Whatever help you need from me . . ." began Strachey.

"Haulin' chore," said Cosmo. "I got stuff needs haulin' from my claim to here."

"I'll arrange it," Strachey said bluntly. "There's nothing you could ask of me, no favor I wouldn't grant. If I have to divert a rig from another run, I'll do it."

"Well now, Ed, I took a look at your big rigs and them fine teamers out back," muttered Cosmo. "And — uh — one rig couldn't do it. Load's kinda heavy. I figure two wagons with six horse teams."

"That means two drivers and two loaders who double as guards." Strachey scratched at his jowls. "Four men for the run. Nothing I wouldn't do for you, old friend, but are you sure we'd need two wagons? You're a prospector. I'm the freight expert, so you'd better let me decide about the weight factor and how many rigs . . ."

"Two," insisted Cosmo. "Try packin' it all in one wagon, the wheels'd get stuck in every soft patch of the trail and the strongest of your team critters'd bust their guts."

"What kind of cargo are we talking about here?" asked Strachey. "I'm assuming you and your niece have decided to resettle in Cooper County and you need a wagon to move your personal effects, furniture, cooking gear, that kind of thing."

"Hell, no," said Cosmo. "We'll resettle, sure, but in Kansas City or Saint Louis. Be here a while, but we'll be movin' on soon as I've tended my business at the bank. That'd be the

Miners National I guess. Big? Got a vault?"

"Biggest in Cooper City and, yes, a strongroom was added some years ago," said Strachey.

"No furniture worth haulin' from the old claim," said Cosmo. "Most of what'll have to be fetched here is the stuff we've mined, and it's some heavier'n feathers, Ed."

"You finally struck it rich?" smiled Strachey. "Congratulations, Cosmo. Never a man deserved it more. Been prospecting ever since the war ended, haven't you?" Cosmo nodded. "I'm glad for you and your niece, but about wagons and crews . . . "

"Two," Cosmo said firmly. "You'll need two. Don't mean to put you to so much trouble, and I can pay for . . . "

"You won't be paying for the services of the Strachey line," countered the freight boss. "Not one cent would I let you pay. Damn it, Cosmo, in all the years since August of 'sixty-three — Paulsen's Ford — there hasn't been a thing I could do to repay you for what you did for me. You could've had anything, a cash loan, a cash gift, anything, but you've never asked, so the debt's still outstanding. If you were a millionaire twice over, I wouldn't take a bent cent from you."

"It wasn't all that much I did," shrugged Cosmo.

"Look at me," urged Strachey. "Here I am, alive and in excellent health, none the worse for my old wounds — thanks to you."

"Yeah, well, officers were important," Cosmo said offhandedly. "We lost Major Grose and Cap'n Doddswell. Couldn't leave Lieutenant Strachey just a'lyin' there, all shot up, could I?"

"You and your Mississippi modesty." Strachey shook his head impatiently. "To this day, you don't seem to realize what you accomplished. Great balls of fire, Cosmo, it was a superhuman achievement. I was a whole lot heavier than you and . . . "

"You were down and hurtin'," argued Cosmo.

"Unable to move, sure, but *you* were wounded too," Strachey reminded him. "A leg wound for the love of Mike. Yet you hung me across your shoulders and carried me — it had to be a mile at least — all the way to the medical aid post, with you dodging everything the Northerners were throwing at us — shells, bullets. And now, so many years later, I'm able to show my appreciation for the first time, and you talk of payment? No chance, Cosmo." Having said all that, he demanded to be told. "What'll we be hauling to Cooper City for you? You said you've mined successfully. Does that mean the cargo will be ore?"

"Well, no," said Cosmo. "Ain't ore. It's the real stuff." He delved into a pocket. "Got a sample to show you. Keep it for a good luck piece if you want. Helluva lot more where it came from. Sacks of it. A whole heap of sacks just a bulgin'."

He tossed it onto the desk. It fell with a thud close to Strachey's right hand and he blinked dazedly.

"Holy suffering . . . !"

"Yup," grunted Cosmo. "That there's a nugget."

Strachey picked it up, tested its weight on his palm, gaped at it.

"Damn and blast," he breathed.

"So now you savvy why it'll have to be two rigs," drawled Cosmo.

After swallowing a lump in his throat and mopping his brow, Strachey asked, "How — how much of it?"

"We got the sacks heaped in the shaft," said Cosmo.

"How big a heap?"

"Lemme think. I'd figure — uh huh — near as high off the ground as I am."

"Hell's bells!"

"Two wagons, Ed. Three spans of teamers apiece."

"By thunder, yes. The strongest we have."

"So what d'you say? Can you oblige

me, Ed? I'd be plumb grateful."

"No question." Strachey was emphatic. "You were wise to come to me. Why, if word of your fortune began spreading . . . "

"Did our best to keep it a secret," Cosmo assured him. "Mary Kate and me."

"Mind putting that thing back in your pocket?" begged Strachey. "This run has to be planned — starting right now — and it's distracting the hell out of me. I have to *think*, Cosmo."

Cosmo retrieved and pocketed the nugget, filled and lit his pipe and waited while his friend put his brain to work. A minute of silence, then Strachey frowned and nodded.

"Got a notion?" prodded Cosmo.

"I hope I can vouch for every man in my employ," said Strachey. "But I can only spare two. Fortunately, they're both drivers with a lot of experience. More importantly, they're tough, they're shrewd and I'd trust them with my life. It's vital, Cosmo, as if I have to convince you, that I assign men whose integrity is unchallengeable. Yes, this is a job I'd assign only to Erling and Worth. Whit Erling is contemptuous of every kind of thief and cheat. His word is his bond. As for Oley Worth, he's a fanatic where honesty is concerned. Nothing could tempt him — not even your fortune. He — uh — tends to be religious into the bargain."

"If you trust 'em, I trust 'em," shrugged Cosmo.

Strachey raised his voice.

"Vern!" The bookkeeper opened the door a moment later and poked his head in. "Find Whit and Oley — on the double."

"Checking harness out back I think," offered Vern. "Be with you in a minute."

Bulky Oley Worth and stringy but just as strong Whit Erling made a favorable impression on Cosmo. They were the kind who look a man straight in the eye while addressing him. He also got the impression they were old cronies. After explaining to Cosmo they'd have to take these two into their confidence and gaining his permission, Strachey tersely did just that. Neither veteran batted an eye nor whistled. Cosmo showed them the nugget. They duly admired it and congratulated him, but that didn't shake them either. First to comment was Erling, who calmly remarked, "I'm glad I'm no blabbermouth. I can keep a secret, and you know you can count on Oley."

"We'll be countin' on the good Lord's help," Worth said piously. "All right now, Mister Strachey, this ain't gonna be like no other run we ever worked. We've hauled all kinds of merchandise, but never nothin' so coveted by the ungodly."

"So we got to do it right," Erling warned his boss, who had risen and was pacing.

"Ed's figurin'," said Cosmo.

"He figures smart," nodded Erling. "Didn't get to head up this business by bein' a slow-brain."

"Strict secrecy, all due care and . . . " Strachey paused to snap his fingers. "Insurance against inquisitive road agents — camouflage!"

"You tell it," urged Erling.

"I'll put you and Oley to work with paint and brushes," muttered Strachey. "White to paint out the line's name — Strachey Freight Company — then black for printing . . . " He paused, then decided, "W.B. Erling, Pots and Pans."

"We can do that," nodded Worth.

"Good figurin'," approved Erling. "Enough pots and pans danglin' and clunkin' inside the rigs to make it sound as true as it looks. Now how about *this*? There's enough lumber in the rear yard for Oley and me to cut planks and put in a fake wagonbed."

"That way, the genuine shipment's out of sight," said Worth. "With the tailgate down, we load the gold at Mister Coote's claim and . . . "

"Cosmo," interjected the little man.

"You boys call me Cosmo, keep it friendly."

"We could lift out the fake bed-planks, load the gold, then fit 'em back in," decided Erling.

"Just what I was thinkin'," said Worth.

"Cosmo, you have a mind-picture of your cache and you've seen our wagons," said Strachey. "Can the shipment be loaded the way they say?"

"Reckon so," said Cosmo, getting to his feet. "So Whit and Oley'll get workin' on them rigs rightaway."

"Rightaway," said Strachey.

"Knew you'd come through for me, Ed," grinned Cosmo. "So now I'll be headed back — and how long d'you calculate . . . ?"

"Not so fast," chided Strachey. "They'll need to check a map and plan their route to your claim, and you have to help. Weren't thinking of leaving before lunchtime, were you? Iris'd never forgive me if I didn't have you home to break bread with us. She's never even met you, and I've talked of you so often."

"Be right proud to meet your wife," said Cosmo. "Meanwhile, break out a map and gimme a pencil and I'll mark out the trail I rid to here."

"Any towns along the route?" demanded Worth.

"And how good's the trail?" asked Erling. "Mind now, Cosmo, we're talkin' about heavy cargo."

"The only town we'll pass through — we might overnight there — is Gilmore's Ford," offered Cosmo. "I overnighted there, stabled my mount at the biggest livery in town."

"We know Gilmore's Ford, right?" Strachey remarked to his men. "And the biggest livery there is owned by an old friend known to all my crews."

"It was the Tucker place," Cosmo recalled.

"Sure, Gibb Tucker," said Worth. "A good man and a doer of the Lord's work. Methodist I think."

"If we have to overnight in Gilmore's Ford, Tucker's got barns big enough to keep both rigs under cover," said Erling. "Chance for you and the little missy to sleep in hotel beds. Me and Oley'd bunk down by the wagons — and plague take any jaspers come nosin' around on account of we'll be loaded for bear."

"Yes, I was going to suggest . . . " began Strachey.

"We'll be armed," Worth grimly assured him. "And then some."

Cosmo Coote began his return journey 2.30 that afternoon after marking the route for the drivers and taking lunch with the Stracheys in their fine home. He had set all the machinery in motion and was content. A week after his return to the claim, less than a week maybe, the camouflaged wagons would arrive. His and his niece's fortune would be loaded after which they would turn their backs on the old Double C and travel with the wagons to Cooper City to begin a new life.

He was content, but would not have been had he suspected his departure from the claim had been noted and reported to a boss-thief planning a hijack.

* * *

The shadows of afternoon were lengthening, the day the old prospector sighted his claim again. He was at first dismayed, seeing two strange horses sharing the corral with the filly and the mule, seeing a stranger squatting crosslegged in the shaft entrance with Rufe curled in his lap, seeing a second stranger lounging by the shack doorway, nursing a Winchester. But then Mary Kate emerged from the shack, waving to him, and the dog scrambled off Stretch's lap and ran toward him, barking a greeting, and he knew all was well at Double C.

He kept the calico moving with Rufe strutting importantly a few feet ahead, leading them in, and glancing to the corral again. The strange horses were a sorrel and pinto. The man rising and ambling clear of the shaft was six and a half feet tall, his loins girded by a double-holstered shell-belt. Small wonder his niece was smiling. The same Texans who had come to her aid in Tyson had taken up temporary residence here, and that was fine by him.

"Uncle Cosmo, say howdy to . . ." she began as he reined up.

"I know who they are, honey, and I'm right thankful to see 'em," he declared.

"Told you he knew all about you, didn't I?" she reminded the tall men.

Cosmo dismounted.

"Valentine — Emerson," he nodded.

"Larry and Stretch," she corrected with a grin.

"Mary Kate trusts us, Cosmo," offered Larry. "We hope you trust us as much, because we've been settin' guard on what's cached in your mine — and we know it ain't pine cones."

"Here to help," explained Stretch. "Seems to us you're gonna need all the help you can get."

"You've travelled quite a piece," said Larry. "Best you get your rest. I'll take care of your horse."

"Supper's comin' right along," announced Mary Kate. "We'll eat early tonight, then you can tell us about Cooper City."

The old man went to his sleeping place to change to his work clothes. Larry saw to the calico's comfort and till the girl was ready to dish up supper, hung around the shafthead, freeing his partner to patrol the area as had been their routine for the past several days.

Cosmo, his niece and Stretch ate in the kitchen, Larry sitting in the shack doorway, plying his fork, listening to the old man's account of his Cooper City visit and keeping his eyes peeled. The feeling had been with him, with his partner too, since their arrival here; they were sure the claim was being kept under observation.

"Sounds good, huh runt?" Stretch suggested when Cosmo finished talking. "It'll look like we're travellin' along with a peddler's rigs."

"So you boys're comin' along," Cosmo was encouraged by this thought. "I'll be mighty obliged. Wasn't for you, there'd only be Mary Kate and me and the drivers. Too bad half of Ed's outfit're still weak from that consarn sickness."

"Influenza," mused Larry. "Flu they call it for short. Really lays folks low, like a fever. When it quit, you don't feel healthy again rightaway, takes time to get your strength back. Good men, Oley Worth and Erling, huh Cosmo?"

"Ed swears by 'em, and he sure knows men," declared Cosmo. "Back in the war, he was a good officer."

"Won't be travellin' fast," Larry reminded him after downing another mouthful. "Not with the weight of the cargo and the mule and the horses tied back of the second rig. Some of the way, we'll ride escort, Stretch and me, but we can spell Worth and Erling at the drivin' chores. We've handled six-horse teams many a time, haulin' big rigs."

"Then there's the other necessaries we got to tote," said Stretch. "Provisions for us and the drivers, feed for sixteen horses and the mule." The dog stopped eating in his corner and turned to stare at him. "Oh, sure. You too, Rufe."

"Never did figure on rollin' fast from here to Cooper City," Cosmo assured them. "What matters is gettin' there. I won't be easy of mind till the gold's stashed in the bank vault and some assayer-feller's through calculatin' what it's worth to us in cash money." When they were through eating, drinking coffee, he frowned at the tall men and muttered, "I guess Mary Kate told you of the marauder me and Rufe sent runnin'."

"She told us," nodded Larry. "And I've wondered, like you've probably wondered, if he spotted your cache before Rufe got to growlin'."

"Sure wish I knew, one way or the

other," winced Cosmo.

"You mean, if he saw it and told somebody else . . . ?" began Mary Kate.

"That's what I mean," said Larry. "Cosmo, ridin' to Cooper City and back, you passed through a lot of lonesome territory?"

"A lot," replied Cosmo. "Man can travel a whole day and sight nary a livin' soul, not even distant smoke of a campfire or a chimney. Might be cattle spreads 'tween here and there, but I saw no strays. Gilmore's Ford now, that's a good town, but it's the only one we'll pass through. I'm guessin' what's in your mind and Mary Kate might's well hear it. It could be we'll have to fight off a raidin' party. I don't relish gettin' ambushed, but it could happen."

"You met your drivers, Oley and . . . ?"

"Whit."

"Yeah. Whit. Two of Strachey's best men, you said."

"Right. And they'll be armed."

"So . . . " Larry nodded encouragingly. "We'll be a well-heeled half-dozen. Any trouble comes our way, I reckon we can handle it."

"Helps if you get a hunch," offered Stretch. "If Larry and me get lucky — and we often do — no bandido'll catch us by surprise. Been many a time we've guessed there was trouble ahead. Sometimes we can durn near smell it."

"Sure." The old man nodded understandingly. "Trouble-shooters' hunches."

"But we'll rely on more than hunches," said Larry. "Keep our eyes peeled, stay curious about any place riders could be hidin', and watchin' the trail. Rockmounds, brush, a stand of timber, any kind of hidin' place."

"Till such places're far behind of us," drawled Stretch.

Mary Kate drained her cup and set it aside — Rufe's signal to quit his corner and jump into her lap. She patted his head and grinned at the Texans.

"We can count on Rufe, too," she

assured them. "Real keen snoot he's got. If the wind's blowin' our way, he'll catch the scent of any other two-legged critters waitin' around."

"And he'll let us know," declared Cosmo. "He's a dog don't bark for no reason."

* * *

Boyd Trenkler returned to the Ortner headquarters 7 o'clock that evening after being relieved by Zeke Pitch. He was hungry by the time he'd corraled his horse. At the cookfire tended by Darrow, he heaped a tin plate from the pot, helped himself to a fork and, after breaking his fast with a mouthful or two, made for the main cabin where Ortner and Merrill were in conversation. He invited himself in, set his supper on the table and drew up a chair.

"Better I eat in here," he said, raising his laden fork. "The old packrat's back, but that ain't all I got to tell you."

"When'd he show?" demanded Merrill.

"Little while before sundown," said Trenkler.

"Just rode in alone?" asked Ortner. Trenkler's mouth was full; he nodded. "All right. It's a safe bet he arranged for transportation of his fortune. We can expect mules or vehicles from Cooper City in a few days, then the gold will be on its way east — and so will we. We'll have a long start on them of course, and ample opportunity for setting up an ambush." He eyed Trenkler expectantly. "What else did you want to tell me?"

"Them strangers at the Double C claim . . ." began Trenkler.

"We know about 'em," shrugged Merrill. "The other lookouts spotted 'em. Maybe Coote's hired 'em to ride escort. Well, they'll be no problem. Only two of 'em."

"Today, I studied 'em careful through the spy-glass," Trenkler frowned. "Nobody else recognized 'em?"

"Should they have?" challenged Ortner.

"Well now, Max, many a jasper of our kind knows of 'em — heard of 'em or saw their pictures in newspapers," said Trenkler. "I sure have, and I got no doubt who they are. Ever hear of a couple Texas do-gooders name of Valentine and Emerson? They've been around a long time — and damned if I savvy why they're still alive."

Merrill swore explosively; Ortner took the news calmly.

"*Them* two!" scowled Merrill. "They meddle, Max. They butt into what's none of their business and raise a lot of hell for the likes of us."

"I'm aware of their reputation," Ortner said coolly. "Can't say I'm particularly impressed. Most of what I've read of them is too far-fetched to be believed. We should be sceptical of the frontier press. Reporters and their editors tend to exaggerate the facts out of all proportion. It's called sensationalism."

"You ever tangle with 'em, Boyd?" demanded Merrill.

"No," said Trenkler. "But I can tell you what happened to many that did. They ended up in some prison — or some trail-town Boot Hill."

"So they've been lucky," shrugged Ortner. "But they're only human. No man's lucky streak lasts forever."

"Max, if they're gonna ride escort on Coote's gold, they better be our first targets," opined Merrill. "We oughtn't take chances with the likes of them."

"Well . . ." Ortner grinned callously. "They're expendable and their sudden demise will have a demoralizing effect on Coote and the others."

"More waitin' now, huh?" mumbled Trenkler, still eating.

"Surveillance will be maintained," nodded Ortner. "When their transportation arrives, we'll begin our run east to find a suitable site for an ambush. Meanwhile, Clay, you'll relay this order to the men. We'll be an anonymous raiding party. Every man must be unidentifiable. That means hoods. We improvise, understand? Dominoes, Clay. Gunnysacks will do. Eye holes of a size to give us clear vision. They'll be pulled on tightly, tucked into our collars and held down by our hats."

"Dusters or slickers too?" suggested Merrill.

"Yes," nodded Ortner. "A complete cover-up, bodies as well as faces. See to it."

Having cleaned his plate, Trenkler licked his thick lips and remarked with relish, "Jesse spotted a whole heap of the stuff in Coote's mine. Hell, we're takin' the jackpot this time. We all end up with a fortune!"

"A great loss to the old man," Ortner dryly remarked. "But, as I said before, riches are wasted on men of his years. Our need is greater."

He changed his strategy five days later. Having given considerable thought to the subject of the Coote cache, he decided he should be absolutely sure it would be shipped to Cooper City. They could be cunning, he warned himself, old prospectors who amassed a fortune after long years of lonely endeavor. The means of shipping the gold would no doubt arrive from the east, but was that any guarantee Coote intended taking it to Cooper City? The old fox might just as likely head north for Melgosa, while he and his men waited in vain at some stake-out along the trail east.

On the fifth day, the man on lookout duty, Ritchie Boneen, sighted moving dust a good distance east of the high country and prepared to use the spyglass provided by his leader. When the two wagons appeared, he focussed on them, studied the plodding teams, the drivers and the freshly painted inscription on the canvas canopies. He grinned derisively. Who did those freighters think they were fooling?

As ordered, he quit his post, made his way back to where his horse was hidden and rode to the Ortner mine.

The coming of the wagons was reported to Ortner and the other men.

There were grins of venal anticipation on every face but Ortner's.

"This is what we been waitin' for," Merrill reminded him.

"Their transportation is arriving as I expected," muttered Ortner. "But it's too early for us to move out. I've reconsidered. It would be quite a frustration, Clay, were we to be in position somewhere along the east trail — unaware the shipment was *not* bound for a Cooper City bank."

"I thought sure he'd . . ." began Merrill.

"So did I," said Ortner. "But maybe he's remembering the night he took a shot at a marauder, maybe he suspects Rodd ventured into his shaft and saw the gold before he was scared off. I have to be certain they'll make for Cooper City, not Denver or Melgosa, and there's only one way."

"We don't move till the shipment leaves," guessed Kaye.

"Exactly," nodded Ortner. "So I'll rely on you, Clay."

"Yeah, all right," shrugged Merrill. "Let me have that spyglass, Ritchie." Before making for the corral to saddle his horse, he assured Ortner, "When I get back, you'll know where they're headed. And, if it's east . . ."

"Time will still be on our side," Ortner said confidently. "Eight riders can move a great deal faster than heavy laden freight wagons."

Rufe began growling, rehearsing a barked challenge, as soon as the rigs were audible.

"Friendlies," Mary Kate called to him, as her uncle came out of the shack and the Texans got to their feet. "Uncle Cosmo?"

"Yup, this'll be them," he grinned.

There was just space enough for the drivers to guide the teams onto the scene and make a half-circle to stall the heavy rigs with their rear ends a short distance from the shafthead. The Texans nudged their Stetsons off their brows and stood arms akimbo, trading amused grins.

"Howdy again, Cosmo," nodded Erling, dropping to the ground. He winked at Mary Kate. "If you need pots or pans, little lady, I'll make you a good price."

"What d'you say, Cosmo?" challenged Worth.

"If I didn't know better, I'd take you boys for a couple dude peddlers," declared Cosmo.

Ed Strachey had spared no expense. The outfits worn by the drivers matched the inscription on the canopies. They looked like itinerant hawkers in their dapper town suits, flashy vests and tan derbies, if somewhat more formidable than most. Of the two, Worth was first to recognize the tall men.

"Hallelujah!" he exclaimed. "Hey, Whit, look who's here and larger'n life!"

4

Action After Dark

COSMO performed introductions. Trading handshakes with Worth and his partner, the Texans noted part of their armory. Both drivers packed holstered .45s and second pistols jutted from their pants-belts. Erling announced that a Winchester and shotgun were stashed behind both wagon-seats, indicated he knew Larry and Stretch by reputation and eagerly enquired,

"You hot shots travellin' along with us?"

"All the way to Cooper City, Whit," nodded Larry.

"We'll be there to help pack Cosmo's gold in that bank vault," promised Stretch.

"I don't feel so bad about it now,

Whit," enthused Worth. "Us with no sidekicks along. Couldn't hope for better helpers, could we?"

"Speakin' of help, we don't have to ride escort every mile of the way," offered Larry. "We can spell you boys, give you a break from your drivin' chores."

"You can handle these teams?" asked Erling.

"Any kind of team," Stretch assured him, "pullin' any kind of rig."

"Best get down to business now," urged Cosmo. "What time you got, Larry?"

Larry fished out his watch.

"Quarter after five. Be sundown pretty soon."

"So I'll get to my cookin'," decided Mary Kate. "Hope you gents got an appetite. Second-last supper I'll be fixin' on that old stove and, come sun-up, last breakfast."

After the girl hurried into the shack, Worth frowned at the shafthead and suggested to Cosmo, "We'd best take a look at the cargo now, calculate how to spread the weight even, then we'll unhitch and feed our teams."

The trouble-shooters didn't tag Cosmo and the drivers into the tunnel. They stayed by the wagons, warily scanning the surrounding terrain.

To the freighters, it was just another cargo to be loaded and hauled, its weight shared by both rigs. There were no startled gasps nor did their eyes dilate after Cosmo lit a lamp to reveal his cache; they could have been planning the loading of drygoods, ironmongery, kegs of whiskey or barrels of beer, anything but a king's ransom in sacks of raw gold.

"How's it look to you, Oley?" asked Erling.

"Divided even, I figure we can fit the stuff into the real wagonbeds," muttered Worth. "Won't pile 'em. We'll line 'em in regular rows both sides so the fake bed'll fit over 'em. Cosmo, it's your consignment. Up to you when we load."

"Gonna be plenty moonlight tonight," said Cosmo. "How about after supper? You'll be boneweary by the time the last pokes packed, so everybody sleeps till sun-up and we start for Cooper City right after breakfast — how about that?"

"Best way," agreed Erling. "Earlier we get goin' the better, because it's for sure we won't make a lot of speed. We'll make the miles, don't you fret, but rollin' steady."

"All right now, we got critters to unhitch and feed," said Worth, leading them out.

Later, when Mary Kate filled and distributed plates, the men ruled against trying to crowd into the tiny kitchen. They squatted in a semi-circle by the shack doorway, plying their forks, approving the girl's satisfying cuisine, catching up on talk. The freighters were deferring to Larry, creating the impression he should assume command, but he gently pointed out,

"Comes to freightin', you jaspers're

the experts. My partner and me, we'll be along for the ride and to help any way we can. If anybody's gonna boss this outfit, it ought to be Cosmo."

"Might seem that way," frowned Cosmo. "But supposin' now there's danger ahead for us, we run into a shootin' fight for instance?"

"Comes to that kind of action, you and your partner're the experts," insisted Erling.

"You two have lived hard, known great perils, spilled blood in your own defense and enjoyed the Lord's protection," Worth gravely reminded them. "My thinkin' is, at the first smell of trouble, we'd better be ready to jump to your orders, Larry Valentine."

"It's not for no reason you and Stretch been settin' guard ever since you rode out from town," murmured Mary Kate. "Ain't none of us forgettin' that snooper."

"And I still can't swear he didn't get inside the shaft and see my cache," muttered Cosmo.

"Well," shrugged Larry. "Best not trouble trouble till trouble troubles us. When we quit this place and start east, if we all stay sharp, I figure we'll take care of ourselves good — ourselves and what's in the wagons."

Supper finished and the coffeepot empty, the men smoked a while. Mary Kate retreated into the shack. When she reappeared, she was rigged in a poncho, donning her headgear and hefting her rifle; the Texans noted she had used cord to improvise a sling for the weapon.

"Best I kind of patrol around while you're loadin' up," she said casually.

The drivers frowned. Cosmo assured them, "You don't have to worry about her. She's sharp-eyed and plenty smart, looks out for herself real good day or night."

She issued a command to Rufe as he prodded at her moccasined feet with his nose.

"You stay, Rufe. And remember . . . " She directed the dog's attention to

Worth and Erling, "they're friendlies."

The girl was lost from view by the time cigarette and cigar stubs were ground out and dottle tapped from pipes. Out of consideration for Cosmo's age, the Texans and the freighters insisted he supervise; no need for him to tote any sacks from the shaft. Worth and Erling cleared the wagons of pots and pans and the planks of the false wagonbed and the loading began.

Larry and Stretch did a lot of lifting and carrying, but left the stashing of the precious sacks to the drivers. In the moonlight and peeled down to pants and undershirts, the men toiled steadily, sweating, never pausing. Sensing the Texans had his niece on their minds, Cosmo forewarned them.

"Don't fear for her if you hear a shot. Fear for the snooper she's shootin' at."

The lofty vantagepoint, a high branch of a tall pine, was reached by agile Mary Kate with little or no muscle-strain. At this height, much of the area beyond the timber was visible to her. Her rifle was cocked and she was comfortable enough, perched where the branch jutted out from the trunk.

From away to the south, carrying clear on the night air, she heard a horse whinny, a distant sound, but not to be ignored. She kept her gaze turned in that direction. Almost thirty minutes passed before she detected stealthy movement. The marauder was too far off to be identified, wasn't even upright.

'Crawlin',' she reflected. 'Bellyin' along from rock to rock like a snake.'

She couldn't hope to draw a clear bead, but could certainly offer discouragement. She deemed that necessary, because it was obvious the man was manoeuvering to approach the claim. Slowly, she nudged the rifle stock into her shoulder and took aim.

When she squeezed trigger, Merrill swore bitterly. With the echo of the shot, the slug ricocheted off a boulder inches from his right shoulder. Had his head not been bowed, chips and grit would have struck his face instead of spattering his broad-brimmed hat. He hugged ground a moment, swore again, then rolled to put that boulder between himself and the sharpshooter.

Stretch froze in the act of passing a sack to Worth.

"Keep loadin'," he heard Cosmo say calmly. "All that shot means is she's fazed some varmint."

"Feels damn peculiar, huh runt?" complained Stretch, as Worth took the sack from him. "Any other such situation, we'd strap on our hardware and hightail it to where she's at, back her up." No rejoinder from Larry, just a soft chuckle. "What's so funny?"

"Dogs're comical critters," grinned Larry. "Look at Rufe there. He's just floppin', watchin' us toil — and pantin' louder'n any of us."

"I noticed," nodded Worth. "Kind of in sympathy with us."

"Uh huh," grunted Erling. "That's what it is. He can't help with the totin', but he figures *that* helps, him pantin' like he's toilin' right along with us."

Cautiously, Merrill began rising. Another shot. This time he spotted the gunflash in the instant before he ducked and heard the bullet strike another rock.

'Shootin' down at me from way up high,' he mused. 'Up a tree most likely. All right, now I got to make him believe I've quit.'

He turned and, on hands and knees, began working his way southward to where he had left his horse tied. Mary Kate levered another shell into the breech and kept her ears cocked. Merrill crawled until he deemed it safe to rise and move on afoot. Later, reaching his mount, he slipped his rein, swung astride and rode a short distance, deliberately covering rocky ground. The wind was blowing from the south. He wanted the sharpshooter to hear receding hoofbeats; all part of his plan.

When he came to softer ground and

high country brush, he slowed his pace, walking the horse into a clear patch where it could not be spotted in daylight — not even from up that damn tree. He dismounted, re-tied the animal and took the telescope from his saddlebag.

'Two can play the same game,' he assured himself. 'I don't have to risk a slug in my head. All that matters is where they're headed. Fine. When they move out, *I'll* be up a tree.'

He did not retrace his steps, but took off in another direction. There were other stands of timber hereabouts and, if he could climb high enough, he needed only to wait for daybreak. Some time after dawn, those wagons would roll. And he would be watching.

The last sack had been loaded. Now, Cosmo and the Texans watched the drivers set the planks of the false wagonbeds back into position. This was done with ease, thanks to the care with which they had packed the sacks.

"Flat as the real bed," bragged Erling. "Not one board out of line, which'd be a dead giveaway."

"Now we load the fake merchandise back in," muttered Worth, "and that's all for tonight. Sufficient unto the day, boys."

Larry moved to his dumped gear to retrieve and strap on his Colt and take up his rifle.

"Time for me to find Mary Kate and send her back here, then I'll stand the first watch," he announced. "Oley, Whit, where'll you bunk?"

"Inside the rigs," Worth told him.

"Bueno," grunted Stretch. "I'll be under a rig. Runt, you come wake me soon as you . . ."

"Sure," nodded Larry. "Soon as I'm too beat to stay sharp-eyed."

"Guess I'll call it a day," mumbled Cosmo. Half-way to the shack, he paused to glance to the shaft and remarked, not wistfully but triumphantly. "My last night sleepin' here."

Guided by his memory of the girl's

two shots, Larry moved through the timber, calling to her.

"Don't shoot at *me*, honey. You can quit now and get your sleep — and climb down careful, hear?"

She answered him a few minutes later. He waited at the base of a pine, not looking up, just listening to the sound of her descent.

"I'm comin' down as careful as I can," he heard her assure him.

"Good girl," he approved. "Beats takin' a long fall, maybe breakin' your neck."

She dangled from the lowest branch and dropped lithely. He steadied her with his strong arms and, with an impish grin, she asked, "Would you pine and fret if I got hurt — like some feller courtin' me?"

"It'd worry me — a lot," he told her. "But not like it'd worry some feller courtin' you. Stretch'd worry too."

"What way then?" she teased.

"Well now, there are a lot of years between us, Mary Kate," he said gently.

"So it'd be the way a . . ."

"The way a big brother'd fret?" she challenged.

He couldn't suppress a grin.

"I said a *lot* of years," he reminded her. "More like an uncle'd fret for you."

"Hogwash," she giggled. "You're as young as you feel."

"Did you have to say that?" he grouched. "I'm just through helpin' load all the gold you and Cosmo mined here. Right now, I'm beat. Young as I feel? I feel like today was my hundredth birthday. Scat now. Get your sleep." She made to move away. He restrained her, grimacing in exasperation. "Damn. My brain must be as weary as my carcass. I didn't ask about them shots you fired."

"Had to be another snooper," she said. "But he's through snoopin' for tonight, might be bleedin' some."

"But you couldn't swear you scored on him."

"No. He was too far off. Wasn't

for the moonlight, I'd never've spotted him. He was crawlin' our way, but far south. I fazed him good. Kept listenin' careful and, sure enough, he took off. I heard his horse."

"All right. Happy dreams, kid."

Long after the girl left him, he stayed awake and alert by prowling the timber and the area north and west of Double C. His steps dragged. He well realized, if he obeyed the urge to squat and rest, he would sink into slumber.

Not until his eyelids felt like lead weights did he return to the claim and flop to his knees by the wagon under which his partner snored. One touch was all it took to rouse Stretch, who rolled out from under, donned his Stetson and reached for his rifle.

"Any action, runt?" he mumbled.

"Dead quiet all around," yawned Larry. "But . . . "

"Sure," grunted Stretch. "Eyes peeled, ears cocked. See you for breakfast."

The taller Texan maintained his

vigilance until sun-up, when Mary Kate was first to stir. The clatter of her breakfast preparations brought her uncle, the drivers and Larry alive to trudge to the spring and perform their ablutions. Worth and Erling then began harnessing their teams supervised by Rufe, the epitome of canine curiosity.

It was a satisfying breakfast. While eating, the old man and his niece kept their backs turned to the shaft, neither of them acknowledging they were about to leave forever what had been home and the scene of their labors for so many years, until Erling casually enquired, "You gonna miss the old place?"

Mary Kate munched and shrugged and let her uncle answer; he took his time about it.

"Some things we'll miss maybe," he said. "Huntin' was always good hereabouts and Mary Kate got to be some fine cook."

"Can't be no argument about that," mumbled Worth, eating with relish.

"Might be we'll miss the excitement too," Cosmo continued. "When a man's been a fossicker for near twenty years, mostly diggin' just a few dollars worth of the yellow, it's like magic when he hits one pay-vein after another and starts cachin' raw nuggets, minin' a fortune. Don't reckon Mary Kate and me could ever forget that feelin'. But what we *won't* miss is the toilin' and sweatin' it took to get all the gold out of them rock walls." He glanced at his niece. "Right, child?"

"Hard work never hurt me none," she bragged.

"No, you never complained about it, but it was wrong," insisted Cosmo. "No life for a purty girl."

"You can make it up to her now," Stretch said encouragingly.

"Durn right," nodded Cosmo. "Got plans for her. We'll travel from Cooper to Kansas City in style. If we don't like Kansas, we'll settle in Saint Louis. Then we'll see to her schoolin', smooth her rough edges, make a lady of her. I aim to hire a teacher just for her."

"What they call a private tutor," nodded Erling. "Yep, that'd be fittin'."

Wrongly assuming that plan had no appeal for Mary Kate, Larry assured her, "That'll be great for you, honey. You're smart, so you'll learn fast. Before you know it, you'll be the most fashionable young lady in town."

"Can't happen too soon for my likin'," she enthused. "The last few years, ridin' into Tyson to trade for supplies, I started envyin' some of the ladies I saw, their purty duds, the way gents tipped their hats to 'em. A tomboy's what Sheriff Hill calls me. I guess that's what I am, but I don't crave to be a tomboy all my life, Larry. What Uncle Cosmo wants for me is what *I* want for me."

"Kid's smart," Erling remarked to Worth. "Knows what's good for her."

"We've been loners too long," declared Cosmo. "I was never meant to be no hermit anyway. City livin's just right for me and the girl. We're friendly.

We like folks. I plan on buyin' us a fine home, hirin' a cook and a housekeeper, buyin' us a fine surrey with a couple of thoroughbreds for us to ride around in. And we'll invite folks to our home. We're gonna be plumb social."

Worth nodded and grinned. Erling drained his cup and announced,

"We'll roll soon as you're ready. Just load what you want to take along and we'll be on our way."

The Texans saddled their mounts. With packrolls, saddlebags and sheathed Winchesters secured, they led the sorrel and pinto out of the coral. Stretch tied the mule back of the second wagon and eyed Cosmo and niece enquiringly.

"You can tie my horse too," said Cosmo. "I'll keep Whit company."

"Guess I'll ride along with Stretch a ways," decided Mary Kate. "Up, Rufe."

The dog leapt into her arms and was lifted over the tailgate of the second rig. Larry helped load the residue of the old man's provisions and his and the girl's few keepsakes, then stepped up to leather. Having tied the mule and the calico, Stretch mounted and watched Worth climb to the seat of the first wagon, Erling and Cosmo to the second.

"I guess that's it, huh?" said Larry, touching a match to his after-breakfast quirley. Everybody nodded. "Bueno. For starters, I'll ride point. Let's go."

Through the spyglass, from his lofty vantage-point, Merrill followed the progress of the wagons and outriders long enough to confirm the direction they were taking. He chuckled as he descended the pine, but did it carefully, loath to risk mishap. No fun hijacking a fortune in gold with an arm in a sling, unable to work a rifle or six-gun.

After dropping to the ground, he half-walked, half-ran southward to his waiting horse. It was a little more than ninety minutes later when he rejoined his companeros to report, "They're rollin' east, got to be makin' for Cooper City."

Ortner nodded complacently.

"Saddle up. Pack all gear, including provisions. Keep hoods within easy reach. We leave rightaway and should pass the wagons in an hour or so, which means we could be taking the gold this very day."

So two mining sites were abandoned this morning, first Double C, then the Ortner mine. Ortner led his band eastward to travel rough country a full mile south of the east-west trail. Rough though it was, the terrain could be covered by horseback without difficulty; they made the miles at speed that couldn't be matched by heavy-laden wagons.

After the first half-mile of their journey, Oley Worth suddenly hauled back on his reins, applied his brake and ordered his fellow travellers to climb down. Larry wheeled his sorrel and idled it to the first wagon, trading puzzled frowns with Stretch. Mary Kate's eyebrows were up, her uncle rising from beside Erling, who winced impatiently.

"Somethin' wrong?" Larry demanded. "Teamer about to throw a shoe?"

"Everybody out and on your feet!" commanded Worth, as he climbed down. "By Henry, I'm ashamed of myself. *Me* — forgettin' somethin' so important!"

"Left somethin' back at the claim?" asked Stretch.

"It should've been done back there before we started out," fretted Worth. "May the good Lord forgive me."

"Oh, sure." Only Erling, so long a crony of Worth's, caught on. He nodded knowingly as he and Cosmo descended. "All right, Oley, get it done."

Dismounting with the Texans, the confused Mary Kate wanted to be told, "Get *what* done?"

Rufe dropped from the second rig unaided, relieved himself against a rear wheel and ambled forward to join the party.

"Before we start a long haul, Oley always prays some," explained Erling.

"Oh," shrugged Stretch.

"It's important," declared Worth. "'Less we're all heathens, we know we can't do a doggone thing, eat or sleep, make a long journey, lift a finger even, 'less the Lord wills it. So we gotta beg His help."

"Well, sure," agreed Cosmo.

"Sounds reasonable," nodded Larry.

"Hats off and form a circle," urged Worth.

They followed his example, baring their heads, holding hats to chests. Rufe positioned himself between the freighters.

"All right, Oley," said Erling. "Do it."

Worth raised his eyes and growled out his prayer.

"Heavenly Father, this is me speakin' again. We've begun a journey and we got a lot of miles to travel and we could run into all kinds of danger so, on behalf of all of us, I'm beggin' You to help us along, grant us Your protection, guard us against all perils we're apt to face and deliver us safe to where we're headed. Be plumb obliged if You'd allow no critters come down with colic or bust a leg. They'll be haulin' strong rigs and a heavy cargo. So, if You could mind we don't bust a wheel or an axle, that'd help a lot too. Thank You kindly — in advance."

He paused. Larry asked.

"That all of it?"

"'Fraid not, Tex," sighed Erling.

"Don't put your hats on yet," said Worth. "We'll now sing the hymn 'Lord, Our Guide and Protector,' Whit knows it. Maybe some of you don't. Anyway, you can pick up the tune. There's only seven verses."

He and Whit began singing. The hymn was strange to the Texans, also to Cosmo and his niece. They couldn't join in but, after sixty seconds of Worth's sonorous baritone bawling and Erling's accompanying tenor, Rufe added his voice. He raised his snout, opening his mouth and wailed and bayed. In truth, the sound he produced was not exactly a treat to the ears and distracted the freighters more than somewhat. It got to where the hound's volume exceeded theirs.

"Uh — Oley . . . " begged Erling, and they gave up.

"Yeah, well, the prayer ought to do it anyway," Worth decided. "As for the singin', it's the thought that counts. All right, folks, we're rollin' again."

The drivers and Cosmo redonned their headgear and reboarded. Stretch gave Rufe a boost into the second rig and, with Mary Kate and Larry, remounted, and the journey was resumed, Larry a short distance in the lead, eyes alert.

Perched beside Erling with his rifle resting on his knees, Cosmo grinned wryly and assumed, "Your pardner Oley likely figures Rufe for a heathen."

"First creek we sight, you better

have Mary Kate hide that dog," warned Erling. "Else he'll want to plumb baptize him. Oley's a real pro at the freightin' business, handy with a gun too. But he sure is religious, a real believer."

Stirrup-to-stirrup with Mary Kate, Stretch talked to her like a fond uncle.

"Purty gowns, walkin' and talkin' ladylike, you'll get to be a mighty popular gal. Got good times ahead, honey."

"And that'll suit me fine," she confided. "You know, the only woman duds I got is my nightgown. I don't sleep in Levis. Workin' the mine or huntin' deer, I move easier in this outfit, but I know it ain't proper for city livin'. I can't hardly wait to get purtied up in silk gowns and frills and lace, everything womanlike. Gonna let my hair grow too. I aim to be *real* purty."

"You won't have to try hard," he opined.

"Hey, how come you and Larry

never got married?" she asked.

"Because it'd be a dumb thing to do," was his prompt reply. "Think now, Mary Kate. If we had wives — kids too — how d'you suppose they'd feel if, while they were fixin' breakfast, we strapped on our guns and told 'em, 'Don't cook nothin' for us. We got to saddle up and ride on account of the bank just got robbed or there's rustlers on the loose or bandidos chasin' a stagecoach or whatever?' We tell 'em we'll be gone maybe a week, maybe longer, like a couple of months. Now I ask you, is that any way for a husband to treat a wife?"

"You mean it'll keep on happenin' — like a habit you can't break?" she challenged.

"We're hexed." He could say this fatalistically nowadays. The trouble-shooters had realized the futility of constant griping about the hand dealt them by Lady Luck. "If we ever tried settlin' down, the joke'd be on us. A man oughtn't try doin' what he knows he can't do."

"You know, that's awful sad," she frowned.

"No, it ain't," he shrugged. "Nobody has to feel sorry for us. We're still livin', we can travel any place we please and we got cash enough to get by on. Thousands ain't so fortunate. So why should we complain?"

It was Larry who chose their noon stop, and he won no argument from the trail-wise drivers. The rear riders, Stretch and Mary Kate, had made brief pauses to pick up firewood. There was enough of it for cooking lunch for six humans and a dog right there beside the trail in open country, the only rises, rockmounds and timber in this area better than a mile away, which meant it was impossible for hostiles to take them by surprise.

Ortner's band was, at this time, quite a few miles to the southeast and approaching the slope of a rocky rise the Texans and their companions would not sight before mid-afternoon. The would-be hijackers would find that, from the summit of the rise, they would command a clear view of the trail which would then be fifty yards away.

As they idled their mounts toward the near slope, Ortner scanned the terrain west and assured his men, "We're miles ahead of them, so we've ample time to stake out the top of this rise."

Darrow urged his horse forward to ride level with Ortner and Merrill.

"Boyd's right, huh?" he prodded. "Valentine and Emerson, the trouble-shooters, them tall jaspers sidin' Coote?"

"I'm just as sure as Boyd," said Merrill. "Max's spyglass is a right handy contraption. I saw 'em clear when they quit Coote's claim with the wagons. You gettin' nervous, Joe?"

"Just leery," growled Darrow. "Don't seem natural to me. Them still bein' alive I mean."

"They aren't invincible and they

certainly aren't bullet-proof," said Ortner.

"Lucky's what they are," said Merrill. "The luck's been with 'em a long time — *too* long."

"Legends," Ortner said contemptuously. "I'll always be sceptical of legends. Hickok was a legend, but where is he now? In a six foot hole in the Black Hills of Dakota. And Valentine and his partner are just as mortal. Two well-aimed bullets — exit the Texas Trouble-Shooters."

He called a halt when they reached the base of the rise. Staring westward, Merrill noted, "No chance they'd spot our horses, if you mean for us to leave 'em here."

"And, from up there . . . " Ortner raised his eyes, "we'll be able to watch a mile or more of the trail."

He eased his boots from stirrups. "Horses to be ground-reined."

After dismounting, he broke out his duster and hood. The others followed suit and, moments later, were climbing the slant, hooded, rigged in dusters or slickers and toting their rifles.

Ample cover atop the rise, a generous scattering of boulders varying in shape and size. At Ortner's instructions, each man chose a vantagepoint. Trenkler insisted, when they were in position, "Don't much matter about the drivers, but we better down them trouble-shooters with our first burst."

"First burst?" Ortner chuckled softly. "There'll be only one burst of fire. Our targets will be the so brave outriders. When Valentine and Emerson fall, Coote and the drivers will know they've lost, will know they've nothing to win but the same fate, if they try to make a fight of it. The element of surprise is in our favor. No challenge. We open fire at my command."

"And now," grinned Merrill, "all we got to do is wait for 'em."

5

Keen Ears and Fast Moves

WHEN the travellers killed their fire, packed the cooking and eating gear and moved on, Mary Kate's filly was plodding along back of the second wagon with her uncle's horse and the mule. She shared the seat of the first rig with Oley Worth, nursing her rifle. Stretch rode level with the second vehicle, calmly scanning the land north and south. Larry was again taking the lead, his sorrel matching the slow and steady pace of the teams.

Rufe was content to travel with his chin resting on the tailgate of the rear rig and his eyes on the tied horses and mule as though daring them to earn his disapproval by some fool move, such as trying to pull loose. No such thought entered the minds of those three animals, but Rufe liked to think he was in charge.

"Bet you never believed you'd be haulin' so rich a cargo," the girl cheerfully challenged.

"No, by dad, I never did," drawled Worth. "Whit and me, all of us Strachey hands, I declare we've toted and delivered every kind of merchandise you could name. Plowshares, minin' tools, and all kinds of stuff. Last fall, we hauled a couple Gatlings to the garrison at Fort Yerby."

"What's a Gatling?"

"Gun. A big'un. Throws heavy calibre bullets and terrible fast. Barrels keep turnin' and spittin' fire. No trigger. You turn a handle, kind of. I'll tell you, little missy, if George Armstrong Custer — may him and his troopers rest in peace — had Gatlings with 'em at the Little Big Horn, it would've been the Sioux and the Kiowas that got massacred."

The veteran freighter continued to

regale the girl with his memories of trails travelled and merchandise toted, while the wagons rolled onward in the afternoon sunshine and the Texans surveyed the topography they now approached. Stretch appraised the woody ridge two hundred yards north. Larry, staring ahead, noted the rock-littered hill coming up to the right of the trail. All right, it was just another hill, broad at its near base and obscuring everything south of it save for a line of brush barely visible, but the near base wasn't far from the trail.

With his short hairs tingling, a sensation he had experienced on countless other occasions, he eased his pace to allow the first team to catch up with him.

Following the approach of their intended victims, the hooded riflemen anticipated an easy takeover.

"The outriders," Ortner said quietly. "Aim carefully now."

Darrow, leaning against a rock waited for the riders and rigs to draw level with the rise and got Larry in his sights. All his weight was pressed to the rock. It was sizeable; his weight could not dislodge it. But he moved a knee, the better to steady himself, and that slight movement budged a pebble or two off the outer edge.

The sound was faint, but Larry's ears were tuned and ready for it. He darted a glance to the top of the rise, sighted the stones clattering down the near slope and something else, four inches of a rifle-barrel. At once he whisked his Winchester from its scabbard and bellowed to his companions.

"Ambushers! The rise! Get behind the wagons — muy pronto!"

Worth and Erling promptly stalled their teams and reached behind the wagonseats for weapons. Cosmo and his niece dropped from their perches to take cover behind the rigs and, as the ambushers opened fire, so did the Texans, cutting loose with their rifles while hustling their mounts off the trail to join the others. Worth and

Erling triggered two shots apiece before quitting their seats.

Moving targets are harder to hit. Neither Texan suffered the sting of a bullet, though some came too close for comfort. Then they were out of their saddle and cutting loose at the rocks atop the rise from standing positions, Larry firing over the rumps of the front team's third pair, Stretch balancing atop a wheel. The afternoon air echoed to the clamorous bark of rifles, Ortner and his men firing down at the wagons, five men and a girl directing their shots to the rocks cluttering the hilltop.

During this uproar, Rufe cringed behind the seat of the second rig. He had, when accompanying Mary Kate on hunting expeditions, grown accustomed to the bark of her rifle, but this just happened to be his first experience of a half-dozen such weapons being discharged close at hand. His eyes dilated, he trembled and whimpered while the team animals and saddle horses stamped and snorted.

Ortner was irate. What he had planned as an ambush was fast becoming a fiasco. His men couldn't draw clear beads without exposing at least part of themselves and, if the defenders couldn't sight on clear targets, they could and did wreak havoc with rapid fire, their bullets cannoning off the rocks. Ricocheting slugs whined about the cursing, would-be hijackers, one cutting an inch off Ortner's hatbrim, another gashing Merrill's left shoulder, another cutting through Boneen's hood and tearing a shallow furrow from jowl to cheekbone. When a bullet burned the left sleeve of Ortner's duster, he swore obscenely and acknowledged the obvious.

"The hell with it . . . !" raged Merrill.

"You don't have to say it," muttered Ortner. "We're at a disadvantage here."

"They got the edge on us!" Kaye's voice shook as he mumbled this warning. "While ever they can bounce lead off of these damn rocks. We stay here, one of us'll stop a ricochet — and it ain't gonna be me."

Ortner nudged Merrill.

"Pass the word along. We're retreating to our horses and making for the brush to the south, keeping this hill between us and the trail."

Moments later, pausing to reload his rifle, Larry realized the only shots he could hear were being triggered by Cosmo and the drivers; Stretch and Mary Kate were reloading.

"Hold your fire," he growled. "Everybody stay quiet — and listen."

"You think . . . ?" called Erling.

"Yeah, I think they're quittin'," said Larry. "Listen, and we'll know for sure."

Everybody listened. Worth was subduing the team animals, Cosmo the horses and mule tied behind the second wagon. Then they heard it, the drumming of hooves receding. Automatically the trouble-shooters hurried to their mounts and swung astride. Stretch called to the girl and men to stay put and pantomimed his intention to his partner; he would make for the west base of the rise. Larry nodded and started for the east side.

When they reached the south base, the eight hooded riders were still visible in the distance, hightailing it for the screening brush. Larry hastily sheathed his Winchester and produced his field-glasses. Through them, while Stretch ambled his pinto along to join them, he studied the fast-disappearing riders.

"We spooked 'em, but good," drawled Stretch. "Some bandidos'll never learn, huh? Rocks atop a hill, bad medicine, worst kind of stakeout. They ridin' easy, runt? Was a helluva lot of lead ricochetin' up there. Might be some of 'em leakin' blood."

"No bastard's fallin' off of his cayuse or clingin' to his saddlehorn," muttered Larry, lowering his glasses. "That don't mean none of 'em're hurtin'. Just means they ain't hurtin' bad enough."

As he returned the binoculars to his saddlebag, Stretch stared southward and asked, "You suppose they'll try again?"

"What's their boss thinkin' right now?" mused Larry. They wheeled their horses to round the base of the hill again. "He knows what's in the wagons and he heads up a seven-strong bunch. For a chance at that much gold, a bonanza, yeah, I'm bettin' they'll try again."

"So . . . " Stretch shrugged and grimaced, "the spy Cosmo sent runnin', he must've got into the shaft and spotted the cache."

"That's how it's startin' to add up," nodded Larry.

"Ortner bunch maybe?" prodded Stretch.

"Five'll get you ten," scowled Larry.

He confided this suspicion to Cosmo and the others when they rejoined them, and the old man sighed resignedly.

"Heard of Ortner's mine, never seen him or any of his crew," he said. "I got to believe you're right, Larry. Ever since that night, I've had the mean feelin' the snooper could've seen the heap before Rufe fazed him. He was sure as hell runnin' from the shaft side of our claim when I took a shot at him."

"Don't nobody fret," chided Worth. "Whit and me got our duty. It's a freightin' man's duty to haul and deliver his cargo — *and* protect it."

"Damn right," growled Erling. He studied his companions with some satisfaction. "We got no casualties, none of us even creased. I'm sayin' we done good."

"Only because we had fair warnin'," Cosmo said soberly. "Well, just *enough* warnin'."

"What'd you see?" Erling asked Larry. "How'd they tip their hand?"

"Don't give me more credit than I rate," shrugged Larry. "I was leery of the hill anyway and, when a little rubble slithered down the slant, I looked up and spotted a gun-barrel."

"Ol' Hawkeye Larry," grinned Mary Kate.

No answering grins from the trouble-shooters. There she stood, rifle cradled in her arms, cheery and serene, her demeanor winning their respect and affection, but saddened them too. This child of the wilderness was underprivileged and didn't know it. She had been deprived of a normal upbringing and, in time of dire danger, thought, reacted and fought like a male, showing no girlish apprehension, none of the typical female traits.

Rufe dropped from the rear wagon. Now that he felt safe, now that the crisis was over, he ran a few paces and barked ferociously toward the top of the rise.

Oley Worth waxed businesslike.

"All right, seems plain them sinners know we're haulin' gold and they'll come a'raidin' again but, till they do, we got to make the miles, get rollin' again." He nodded to the Texans. "You boys'll be lookin' out for a safe nightcamp for us, huh?"

"You know it, Oley," said Stretch.

"Got to find a position we can defend."

"One thing I don't savvy," frowned Mary Kate.

"Ask, somebody'll explain, and then we best be on our way," urged Erling.

"We took good cover, so they couldn't get a clear shot at us," she said. "But why didn't they shoot at our horses? By killin' a couple teamers, maybe three, they could slow us down. Why didn't they do that?"

The men traded glances. Patiently, Larry told her, "They wouldn't settle for as much gold as they can pack in their saddlebags. It'd only be a little piece of the shipment, but heavy enough to slow *them* down. Hijackers go for it all, Mary Kate. If they'd won, they wouldn't have unloaded the stuff. They'd have taken the wagons — and the teams to haul 'em."

"Greed is many a man's downfall," Worth grimly intoned.

"Amen to that, Oley," said Stretch.

"C'mon now," Erling said briskly. "We're wastin' daylight."

Cosmo and the drivers climbed to the wagon-seats. Mary Kate whistled Rufe, boosted him into the rear rig, tied her filly with the calico and the mule and climbed in after him. The wagons rolled again, the Texans a few yards ahead of the first team, stirrup-to-stirrup and swapping hunches.

"We gave 'em a bad time, but it'll take more'n that to discourage 'em," opined Stretch.

"While we're travellin' this trail, they're somewheres south of the brush, plannin' their next move," muttered Larry. "I got to say it, amigo. This time out, I'm thankful we ain't bodyguardin' greenhorns. Eight we counted, eight with the gold-greed. We've fought and licked that many, and more, but . . ."

"But this time?" frowned Stretch.

"It's good Oley and Whit're fighters," said Larry. "It's good Cosmo's handy with a rifle and Mary Kate's no squeamish female. Could take all six of us to hold back Ortner's crew."

"I guess it has to be that bunch," nodded Stretch.

"You found the spy's tracks and they led toward the Ortner mine," Larry reminded him. "We know they're trigger-happy. Think of that Kaye hombre, him that took a shot at us just for the hell of it, and the hard cases we saw at Ortner's claim, every one of 'em gun-hung. Sure, my money's on the Ortner gang."

"You're as sure as if you could see right through their hoods," said Stretch. "All right, I guess I'm just as sure. So we know who we're up against, but no use us bellyachin' to the law when we make Gilmore's Ford. We're sure enough, but we got no proof." He started ahead. "For a nightcamp, I wouldn't choose a creekbank. Where there's water, there's greenery, too much cover for marauders. Basin wouldn't be safe enough neither, not even with one of us patrollin' the rim. What d'you say? Some place high?"

"Higher the better," declared Larry.

"And pray for moonlight. Our lookouts ought to be able to watch all the land around."

The water barrels fixed to the wagons hadn't been holed by ambushers' bullets, for a wonder. But, before the party forded a narrow and shallow creek, the riders took the precaution of refilling canteens. Thirst was one drawback they could guard against.

Some twenty minutes before sundown, the Texans gratefully decided on the ideal site for a night-camp. To the northeast, they sighted a flat-top, its summit high above ground level but it's slopes gentle enough for the teamers and saddle animals to climb and, in the morning, descend without great difficulty. The land surrounding it was pooltable-flat and almost devoid of rocks and brush-clumps, so there would be little cover for night raiders attempting a surprise visit.

Responding to Larry's signal, the drivers turned their teams off the trail to make for the flat-top.

* * *

After the eight had disappeared into the brush Ortner led them eastward again. He was satisfied the flesh wounds suffered by Merrill and Boneen did not require immediate attention and could not be drawn into the wrangling of his men; predictably, there was heated argument as to why the ambush had backfired on them, how the first outrider had gotten wise to them. Ortner had his own theory, but wasn't about to air it until he had planned his next move.

He calculated they were many a useful mile east of wherever their quarry was nightcamped when they reached a spring surrounded by spruce and aspen. Gruffly, he ordered that firewood be gathered for cooking a meal and the horses fed and watered.

Not till they were half-way through that austere supper did he begin to talk. Somebody had doused Merrill's gashed shoulder and fixed a rough dressing. Boneen's face smarted from a liberal application of iodine and his mood was incendiary. Trenkler stated emphatically that it was Larry Valentine who warned of their presence atop the rise.

"Big jasper forkin' the sorrel, that's Valentine — the smart one," he growled. "But don't nobody ask me how in blue blazes he caught onto us."

"Lucky guess," scowled Merrill.

"Plainly, Valentine's the more dangerous of the two," said Ortner. "He's intuitive and has sharp instincts. Of course Emerson is dangerous enough when the shooting starts."

"In to — what?" grouched Merrill.

"Intuitive or, as you said, a lucky guesser." Ortner grinned sardonically. "Control your temper, Clay. We suffered a reversal this afternoon, but the gold is still a long way from Cooper City. Next time, we'll succeed, because Coote and those wagon-drivers won't have the Texans backing them. Valentine and his partner will travel no farther than Gilmore's Ford. It's obvious they're our main problem, so they have to be disposed of. We'll be camped a little way south of Gilmore's Ford long before the wagons get there. If we make an early start tomorrow, we could have as much as a forty-eight hour lead on them."

"Them rigs can't make much speed," remarked Darrow. "Not totin' that kinda weight."

"Whether they make a noon stop at Gilmore's Ford or stay overnight, that's as close to Cooper City as the Texans will get," declared Ortner.

"If we're gonna settle their hash in that town, I'm volunteerin'," breathed Boneen, feeling at his face-wound. "I'll carry this scar to my grave, and I owe 'em for that."

"You won't venture into town, Ritchie, nor will there be any gunplay," countered Ortner. "A face-to-face shoot-out could cost me two men. Trying to pick them off from a rooftop or an alleymouth could be just as fatal."

"Right." Trenkler grunted agreement. "It's been tried before and, hell, their luck's plain unnatural."

"Get close and do it quiet," Pitch suggested baring his teeth. "With knives."

"Forget it, Zeke," sighed Merrill.

"I'm startin' to recollect things *I've* heard of them bastards," Kaye said sourly.

"So . . . " Darrow fidgeted impatiently. "We can make Gilmore's Ford far ahead of 'em, but no shootin', no knives, so just *how* do we cut 'em loose from Coote and the freighters?"

"The law authorities of Gilmore's Ford will oblige us by taking them into custody," drawled Ortner.

Merrill and the others eyed him incredulously.

"Hell's sakes!" exclaimed Kaye. "Are you just gonna ride in and ask the sheriff polite-like to lock 'em up?"

"Hardly," said Ortner. "I won't even be seen in Gilmore's Ford. As for the sheriff, he won't have to be asked. A charge will be sworn against Valentine or Emerson — or both — and I'm confident local law officers will welcome an excuse to apprehend them."

"Well, sure," grinned Trenkler. "Most tin stars're jealous as hell of 'em, hate their guts."

"My little plan for putting those trouble-shooters out of action will work whether they over-night or make a noon stop," said Ortner. "The other tactic I've planned . . . " He paused, thought a moment, then shrugged. "I'd waste time explaining it here and now, because it could only work at night. It can wait till we can estimate exactly when they'll reach Gilmore's Ford, late morning, late afternoon, whichever." Now he fixed his thoughtful gaze on Trenkler. "Boyd, you weren't present when Valentine and Emerson brought Leon to our claim."

"Leon sore-nosed," leered Rodd.

"That sonofabitch Valentine!" fumed Kaye. "To think I had him in my sights today! Hell, how I hungered to put a bullet through his head!"

"I was takin' a turn at watchin' Double C," Trenkler recalled.

"Yes," said Ortner. "And picking pockets is one of your talents, isn't it?"

"Pardon me for braggin'." Trenkler slid an arm about the shoulders of the man squatting next to him, Darrow, and patted his chest. "But, if you want proof . . . "

He grinned and exhibited Darrow's wallet, winning an approving nod from Ortner and a curse from Darrow.

"Gimme that!"

"All yours, Joe," shrugged Trenkler, as Darrow snatched for his wallet. "Just demonstratin'."

"The important thing, Boyd, is can you plant a wallet as easily as you can lift one?" challenged Ortner.

"I can do that," Trenkler assured him. "But why would I?"

"You'll be told presently," said Ortner. "Now this ruse calls for two good men. The Texans won't recognize Boyd. So think back to when they were with us at the mine." His gaze travelled from face to face. "There were harsh words. Valentine and his partner did most of their talking to me. How much attention did they pay the rest of you?" He eyed Darrow. "If I remember correctly, you spoke. And you, Clay, made yourself heard, let your temper get the better of you. How about you others? The man who backs Boyd's play has to be the one they're least likely to remember. This is important, so think carefully."

Boneen and Pitch were uncertain, but Jesse Rodd spoke up.

"I was behind Ritchie and Zeke," he offered. "I looked them hot shots over just like we all did, but I'd say they scarce noticed me."

"Then you'll work the set-up with Boyd," said Ortner. "But play it safe. When the time comes, I want you clean-shaven. Borrow somebody else's hat. I'll lend you a clean shirt. Now listen carefully, both of you. Follow my instructions to the letter, say everything exactly as I tell you to say it, and I guarantee those heroes will end up in the Gilmore County Jail. I'll have rid us of two dangerous meddlers."

He dealt out his strategy step by step and, by the time he was through talking, the other men were laughing and Trenkler and Rodd trading knowing nods, confident they would achieve their purpose. Did they have any questions?

"No, seems to me you've figured it good," said Trenkler. "Saloon'd be the best place and, by the time that outfit rolls into town, them heroes'll have quite a thirst. We can do it, me and Jesse."

"What's this other plan you mentioned?" asked Merrill.

"Don't make me repeat myself," chided Ortner. "I already indicated I can't decide about it until the wagons reach Gilmore's Ford. The Texans haven't seen Boyd, so it's safe for him to be in town when they arrive. He'll report to us. Only *then* can I decide. Patience, Clay. If both strategies are used, I'll need a third man in town, and you'll be my first choice. Naturally, you won't get together with Boyd and Jesse till the trouble-shooters are in custody. That's all I'll say about it at this time — so no more questions."

The men bent on acquiring the Coote gold rolled into their blankets soon afterward, anticipating they would make an early start next morning. Merrill saw no need to post guards.

In the nightcamp on the flat-topped hill, the atmosphere was not so relaxed. The supper cooked and dished up by Mary Kate had been eaten and washed down with coffee. There was no disagreement as to the significance of the unsuccessful ambush. Cosmo's fortune was a rich prize. The hooded raiders would strike again; five men and a girl were unanimous. Worth and Erling gave an assurance that, if Larry and Stretch could sit guard till midnight, they would get sufficient sleep, awake refreshed when summoned and stay wide awake till dawn.

"We're used to it," Erling declared. "When a freight outfit camps down nights, drivers and their sidekicks work shifts at settin' guard. Comes as natural to us as you boys."

"Your watches won't be so long if Mary Kate and me take our turn," offered Cosmo. "Hey, I wish you jaspers'd forget I'm some older'n you. Older I might be, but I'm still plenty spry."

Larry placated him by promising that, if any sentry found himself dozing off, he would be asked to take over.

While the others slept, the tall men stayed wide awake and watchful. Larry squatted at the south edge, scanning the area south, while his partner patrolled east, north, west, then along to where Larry nursed not his rifle but a furry bundle. Grinning, he hunkered to stroke Rufe's head.

"Joined me a little while ago,"

muttered Larry. "Just came away from the fire, sniffed his way to me and flopped in my lap."

"Knows we'll do him no harm," remarked Stretch, "on account of Mary Kate called us friendlies."

"He'd've figured it out for himself anyway," opined Larry. "Dogs ain't stupid. They got instincts. We've seen it happen before."

"Time and time again," agreed Stretch.

"Any hombre ain't partial to dogs, apt to cuss 'em or swing a kick at 'em, they stay far clear of him," said Larry. "Any hombre likes dogs, they beeline for him with their tail waggin'. They back their hunches like I do, but they're better at it than I'll ever be. My hunches don't always pay off . . ."

"Well, you're only human," chuckled Stretch.

". . . but critter like Rufe don't make dumb mistakes," declared Larry. "They savvy some people better'n people savvy people."

"What's that sound?" Stretch cocked an ear.

"Rufe," replied Larry. "You're wide awake and so am I, so it has to be *him* snorin'."

"Damned if he ain't," agreed Stretch. "Plumb tuckered out from all his hard toil."

"And with his belly full," said Larry.

"Kind of special, ain't they?" The taller Texan waxed sentimental. "Dogs I mean. Thinkin' about 'em, I can feel sorry for folks that don't like 'em, never study 'em, pay 'em no mind."

"Their loss," shrugged Larry. "I'm sorry for 'em too. They miss out on a lot of laughs."

Like most other canines, Rufe tended to take short naps. He stopped snoring, opened his eyes, yawned noisily and climbed from Larry's lap to saunter back to the fire. Stretch followed him with his eyes, then glanced sidelong at Larry.

"Can't see your face real clear," he said softly. "But I got a feelin' you ain't smilin' right now. Somethin' fazin' you, runt?"

"There's others I'm sorry for," sighed Larry. "Greedy fools like them hijackers."

"You're sorry for *them*?" challenged Stretch.

"Sorry for what greed'll do to 'em — and to any that'll never settle for what they got," frowned Larry. "I can savvy an old timer like Cosmo, or cattlemen or sodbusters gettin' theirs by workin' for it. They get rich, fine, they're entitled, they've earned it. Feel the same way about gamblers, long as they ain't sore losers. But grabbers like Ortner and his bunch, them I'll *never* savvy. They'd kill for what's in them wagons. They're so damn hungry for it, they forget the risks. Could be some of *them* end up dead, maybe *all* of 'em. Hell, don't they care?"

"Best not strain your brain tryin' to make sense of it," soothed Stretch. "You're the one said it, and it's true. For every smart thief or killer, there's a couple dozen or more that ain't smart at all."

Larry grimaced, got to his feet and flexed his muscles.

"You squat a while," he urged. "Time for me to stretch my legs."

He picked up his rifle. Before he moved away, Stretch muttered advice.

"No use gripin' about it, ol' buddy. We both know we'll see Cosmo's fortune stashed in that Cooper City bank — and we both know we're gonna have to tangle with them hard cases again before we get there. That's the way of it."

"Ain't that the truth," Larry moodily agreed.

At midnight, they were relieved by Worth and Erling, didn't have to rouse them. The freighters stayed on watch till 4 a.m., at which time Cosmo and his niece, early risers from long habit, urged them catch two hours more sleep before breakfast.

"Ain't sayin' you boys couldn't stay sharp till sun-up," said Cosmo.

"Just remindin' you it never happened before."

"*What* never happened before?" asked Worth.

"You never hauled a load so valuable," said Cosmo. "I want you bright-eyed and bushy-tailed while we're travellin'. To stay sharp all day, you got to rest your brains and your bones as much as you can."

"Bunk down, gents," urged Mary Kate.

"Hey, you don't have to coddle us," protested Erling.

"Yes we do too," she good-humoredly retorted.

She was still in good humor, her optimism unsinkable, when she ladled food onto plates some thirty minutes after sunrise. Over breakfast, the Texans listened to Cosmo's plans for 'a right fine home' in Kansas City or St Louis while the freighters calculated miles travelled to date and involved themselves in speculation on distance still to be covered.

Mary Kate expressed her eager anticipation of having a hotel room all to herself and sleeping in a regular bed when they reached Gilmore's Ford and was advised by Erling.

"That's somethin' for you to look forward to, little lady, but it won't be all that soon. The rate we're movin', it'll be three and a half days before we roll into the Ford."

"If that soon," frowned Worth. "Could take longer."

"No matter," she smiled. "I got that much longer to relish the idea."

Erling had a grouch.

"It'd help some," he declared, "if we could guess exactly when them hijackers'll jump us again."

"Sure would," Stretch agreed.

"I suppose," Cosmo suggested to Larry, "the only way is keep on doin' what we been doin', travel along steady and watch out for likely stakeouts."

"Right," nodded Larry. "The only way. We sight rockmounds or timber ahead, close by our route, we have to be ready for anything."

Breakfast over, they packed gear, hitched teams, saddled horses and began the descent to the flats and the trail.

For three days thereafter, they travelled wary, making the miles in daylight, choosing campsites in sparsely vegetated areas north and south of their route and, during the hours of darkness mounting double guard posts. And, had they but realized it, these precautions were unnecessary. Not only was Ortner's party giving the trail a wide berth, the desperadoes were many a mile ahead.

It was late afternoon of a high temperature day when Ortner and his men sighted the smoke of the big town north, Gilmore's Ford, so named for its strong timber bridge spanning Culhane Creek. Two hundred yards south of the trail, within a stand of timber, a sizable clearing would be their temporary base, the charcoal-stained ground dead centre of it identifying it as an oft-used campsite. All but

Trenkler dismounted.

"You have your instructions," said Ortner. "But, just to be sure . . . "

"All right, here's how it goes," said Trenkler. "I stable my horse, check into some cheap room and board place and hang around till they show. If they're gonna noon in town, I come back to fetch Jesse. If they're overnightin', Clay comes along with me and Jesse. And I won't forget about the grainsack."

"Clay will have the message for Coote," said Ortner. "From now on, let's all hope it's this time of day when they arrive. That's all, Boyd. Get going now."

The main group began offsaddling and rigging a picketline, while Trenkler rode out of the clearing to start for Gilmore's Ford.

6

The Set-Up

BY noon of the following day, Tucker's Livery & Barn, the biggest establishment of its kind in Gilmore's Ford, was being kept under observation by Ortner's spy. Trenkler ate lunch by a front window of the small cafe directly opposite on the big town's main street, asked himself a question and decided the answer. Where else would the freighters masquerading as peddlers board their teams and rigs during their stay here? No other livery in this town could accommodate freight wagons; the barn was the Ford's biggest and there were two corrals taking up a great deal of space. Obviously, Tucker's place was a local landmark. It's fading red-painted name-sign advertised special service for heavy vehicles. Tucker was himself a wheelwright and there was a forge attached, a blacksmith always available.

'Wouldn't be the first time freighters rested their teams here,' he assured himself.

Sheriff Dave Kelland, long a resident of the county seat, was at this time lunching with his wife and two daughters at his home on Druitt Street in the Ford's middle-class area. He would be in office another three years at least, being a lean veteran and durable, thanks to an even disposition and temperate habits. Self-control was second nature to Dave Kelland, he neither smoked nor drank to excess.

Also at this time, Kelland's junior deputy, Steve Heenan, emerged from the county jail's ground floor cell-block after serving lunch to an almost permanent inmate, a deadbeat who could never win a popularity contest. Well, not as far as the wealthier citizens of the county seat were concerned.

Elmer Walley, when needing to sleep off a long drinking bout, tended to scorn back alleys and haylofts and seek a better class of roost, such as the rear or front porches of the residences of the local upper crust, the lobby of the town's finest hotel, the Occidental, owner Mayor Colfax, a pew of the recently erected Episcopalian Church and, on one memorable occasion, because a window had been left unlocked, the bedroom of the mansion of none other than Chester Flood, manager of the Ranchers National Bank. Though a rumpot, Walley did have his standards.

Re-entering the front office, Heenan noted his colleague, Miles Vockler, was still seated at the second desk, still leafing through a thick file. A drawer of the file cabinet was still open and Vockler, burly and florid, still sneering. Heenan was no youngster, but his status was junior deputy; Vockler just happened to be a year and a half older.

"You read that damn file once every month at least," Heenan remarked, seating himself on the office couch. "With the ugliest look on your kisser, Miles."

"Stay quiet, I'm concentratin'," growled Vockler.

"You're torturin' yourself," said Heenan, with a wry grin. "Keep lookin', but you'll never find what you're searchin' for. There just ain't no warrants outstandin' on them free-ridin' Texans, so you might's well quit dreamin'."

"Some day!" breathed Vockler.

"It don't make sense, your grudge against Valentine and Emerson," frowned Heenan. "Hell, you never even met 'em. You hate their gizzards because they're southerners? I'm a northerner like you, and *I* don't hate 'em."

"Smart-asses," scowled Vockler. "Big heroes, big reputation for makin' lawmen look like useless no-accounts. I pray for it, pray the time'll come when

I can nail 'em, march 'em in here with my shotgun at their backs, prod 'em into a cell and turn the key on 'em!"

"Anybody ever tell you, Miles?" sighed Heenan. "You got a mean streak. You're a mighty spiteful feller."

"Thumbin' their noses at us," mumbled Vockler. "Their names and pictures in the papers. Playin' it brave, roundin' up badmen so all kinds of fool citizens admire 'em for it. *Admire* 'em! And what are they? Drifters, saddlebums, trail-trash!"

"But smart," said Heenan. "Damn near unbeatable. They're still on the loose, but what of the bandidos and cheaters and killers they've fought? Every law-breaker they beat, he's one less for the law to fret about."

"Lucky, not smart," countered Vockler.

"Somethin' like twenty years," retorted Heenan. "That's a lot of luck, Miles."

"I brought in the Dutton brothers a year ago, tracked 'em down, got the drop, brought 'em in single-handed," Vockler sourly reminded him. "I headed up the posse that trapped a half-dozen brand-changers on Buck Judson's range and it was me shot it out with the bastards that robbed McFarlane's store — and won. But how much about me did Bryar print in his newspaper? Just a few lines, not even on the front page. And he didn't spell my name right, damn him. If it'd been Valentine and his buddy did all that, Bryar would've made big news of it."

"I'll bet, if you asked Valentine or Emerson, they'd bellyache about their big reputations, call it a blame nuisance," said Heenan. "Who needs to be famous? What'll it matter when we're all dead and gone?"

"Nobody can guess where they'll show up next." Vockler's eyes gleamed as he closed the file and scratched a match to light the cold half of a stogie. "My time'll come, you'll see. Sooner or later, they'll come ridin' into my territory and I'll watch 'em like a hawk. All I need is for 'em to step out of line — just a little bit — and I'll have 'em in a cell before they know what's happenin' to 'em!" He gestured to the file. "You can put that away now."

Heenan had reserves of patience.

"Yes, *sir*," he grinned, and rose, came to the desk, picked up the thick file and returned it to its drawer. "Glad to oblige — seein' as how you're plumb weary from gripin' about them drifters."

"Don't sass me," growled Vockler. "You're junior deputy here, and don't you forget it."

"By only a year and a half," said Heenan. "I'm no green kid just gettin' into the law business — which is somethin' *you* oughtn't forget."

He was resting on the office couch again 4.30 of the following afternoon, when the wagons and escorts approached from the west. This time, he was horizontal. Scheduled to relieve his colleague at midnight to work the graveyard patrol, he liked to get ample rest in advance. After supper, he would retire to his boarding house room and sleep till 11.45 p.m., relying on his landlady to wake him at that time. Sheriff Kelland was at his desk, catching up on his paper work.

And Deputy Vockler and Boyd Trenkler were out and about.

Rising in their stirrups, the Texans surveyed all they could see of the big town. From beside the driver of the first wagon, Cosmo said with relief, "Gilmore's Ford. Good town for restin' up."

Mary Kate brought her filly up level and began repeating herself.

"I can't wait to . . . "

"Sure, honey," he nodded. "Supper in a hotel dinin' room, a right soft bed. You'll sleep like a baby this night."

Vockler began to believe in the power of prayer when he recognized the tall riders leading the big rigs along Main Street to Tucker's; his pulse quickened. Trenkler rose from a sidewalk bench, ready for some discreet hovering and eavesdropping.

Cosmo and the freighters were accorded a warm welcome by the proprietor. Wiry and affable, Gibb Tucker greeted Worth and Erling by name and was introduced to Mary Kate and the Texans. Ample accommodation for the saddlers and team animals in a corral, he assured them, and no objections to the freighters sleeping in the barn with the wagons.

"Make it the Sherwood Hotel," Erling advised Cosmo. "It's closest, and you'd want to be close, right?"

"*Durn* right," nodded Cosmo.

He, his niece and the Texans were preparing to carry their overnight gear to the hotel when Rufe turned to peer toward the area behind the stable; he sniffed, bayed, pawed ground, then took off.

"Rufe! Come back here!" ordered Mary Kate.

"Young lady, that hound can hear you, but he won't pay you any mind," warned Tucker, grinning and winking at the men. "My guess is you won't see him again till morning, when you're ready to leave."

"Aw, shoot," she frowned. "Is there a bitch in heat hereabouts?"

"More than one," chuckled Tucker. "Doc Latimer's, Mrs Brodie's and a couple others."

"It's said every dog has his day, honey," remarked Cosmo, trading grins with the Texans. "They — uh — they have their nights too."

The trouble-shooters were amused by the alacrity with which Rufe had gone a'wooing. Not till the morrow would they realize there couldn't have been a worse time for the dog to obey his natural biological instincts.

There were a great many pedestrians moving with them and toward them when they walked to the Sherwood Hotel; they had no way of guessing they were being tagged. In the lobby, while they were registering, Trenkler pretended to be absorbed in a framed print of a Currier & Ives landscape. There weren't many vacancies, the desk-clerk announced. If Mister Valentine and his friend wished to be in earshot of the young lady's room, they could have a double, ground floor rear and four doors from hers. The other single was upstairs. Cosmo insisted climbing stairs was no problem to him, so they signed the register, collected their keys and separated to tidy up before supper. There would be time for Mary Kate to spend the money given her by her uncle; she would have purchased and donned a gown by suppertime.

Trenkler changed position long enough to note the location of the room unlocked and entered by the girl, then left the hotel to amble to the livery at which his horse was stabled. He rode out of town soon afterward and did not spur his mount to a run till he was clear of the edge of town.

On his way home, the sheriff encountered his senior deputy loitering in front of the Sherwood Hotel. He paused for a few words.

"Company tonight," he remarked. "We're having the Millers to supper. That means I won't be back in my office till morning. Still, you and Steve can keep the town safe till then."

"Big night for you," suggested Vockler, "if you and Jerry Miller get locked into a chess game."

"And, when my wife and Jerry's get to swapping gossip, they're at it hour after hour." Before moving on, Kelland thought to stress. "But peace-keeping's more important than socializing so, if you or Steve strike heavy trouble, send for me at once."

"Won't have to do that," Vockler assured him. "Have a nice night."

By sundown, Trenkler had reported the arrival of the gold movers and their accommodation arrangements, and Ortner was smelling success.

"Ground floor rear," he grinned at Merrill while handing him an envelope. "Makes it that much easier for you."

"We'll get it done," nodded Merrill.

"But don't be lookin' for us to get back around midnight. It'll be long after. We're gonna have to do it when the town's closed down and everything's quiet."

"You'll leave immediately even so," insisted Ortner. "Boyd has to show you the layout before he and Jesse take care of the Texans." To Trenkler and Rodd he muttered a warning. "Be prepared to spend some time in the sheriff's office. It's entirely possible you'll be required to sign statements. That's the routine when you're swearing charges. Remember now, you co-operate with the law officer on duty."

"And we oughtn't act nervous," frowned Rodd.

"Damn it, no!" snapped Ortner. "We're a long way from Nebraska. How could any lawman recognize you anyway? Every job we pulled, we were heavily masked."

"It'll be okay," Rodd hastened to assured him.

"We'll play it right," said Trenkler.

"Just the way you dealt it out."
"So let's get goin'," urged Merrill.

* * *

Mary Kate had much to learn about dress-sense, but the proprietress of the store she patronized had taken pity on her, helping her select the right item, offering advice, ensuring the garment was a perfect fit. At supper with her uncle and the Texans in the hotel dining room, she was looking her best and drawing compliments. The gown was of simple design and suited her; Cosmo said as much and the tall men warmly agreed.

"Feels good," she confided. "After we're settled, I'm never gonna wear Levis again."

When they were beginning their dessert, Cosmo stifled a yawn and admitted to feeling more than a little weary.

"Only natural," said Larry. "We've travelled quite a ways, Cosmo and you helped guard our nightcamps, ain't been gettin' as much sleep as you need."

"I'll sure sleep deep tonight," Cosmo predicted.

"Me too," smiled Mary Kate. "Hey, you should feel my bed. It's so *soft*."

"No, *we* oughtn't feel it," grinned Stretch. "*You* should. It's *your* bed, honey."

"You boys relievin' Oley and Whit come midnight, huh?" prodded Cosmo.

"Maybe earlier," said Larry. "We'll take a look around town after supper, find us a peaceable saloon and do a little drinkin', but not for long. Likely sleep better'n three hours before we take over from Oley and Whit."

A short time later, after Cosmo and his niece had retired and the trouble-shooters were strolling Main Street, they sighted none of the men interested in their movements. Merrill was guarding three saddle horses in the alley behind the hotel, Trenkler and Rodd tagging them, but at a respectful distance, and Miles Vockler keeping pace with them, walking the opposite sidewalk, toting a sawn-off shotgun and looking every inch the typical patrolling deputy, watching them, but with sidelong glances, not turning his face their way. Once in a while, the sixth sense of the trouble-prone drifters failed them; this was to be one of those times.

The men Vockler so despised entered the Branding Iron Bar. Minutes later, so did two other strangers in town, but Vockler was oblivious to them at this point, totally preoccupied with his intended victims. Rarely any rowdiness in the Branding Iron, he recalled, but he had high hopes.

He crossed the street and, from atop the batwings, saw the Texans bellying up to the bar with Trenkler and Rodd hovering close.

The barkeep was catering to the thirst of an average number of customers; the bar room was neither semi-deserted nor overcrowded. Elbows propped, boot heels resting on the brass rail, the tall men drank rye and conversed quietly. Positioned at the taller Texan's right side, Trenkler pretended to lose his balance while reaching for his drink; for a brief moment he slumped against Stretch, who promptly chided him.

"Easy, feller."

"Sorry," grunted Trenkler. "My fault."

"No harm done," shrugged Stretch.

Trenkler and Rodd drank deeply. The barkeep eyed them impatiently and Trenkler apologized again.

"Sorry. Forgot to pay for our shots."

"You got an honest face," grinned the barkeep. "But you know how it goes. Most jaspers put money on the bar when they order."

"Have to ask you to change a ten," said Trenkler, his right hand moving to his hip pocket.

"I can do that," said the barkeep.

A startled gasp from Trenkler. Rodd picked up his cue and glared accusingly at Stretch.

"I've been robbed!" Trenkler loudly

complained. Vockler heard and came bounding through the entrance, cocking his shotgun and grinning hopefully. "Some sonofabitch lifted my wallet!"

"And I'm guessin' who," growled Rodd.

"I had it when we came in!" raged Trenkler.

"Had to be the beanpole," declared Rodd. "You got too close to the pocket-pickin' skunk."

"Just what the hell're you tryin' to . . . ?" began Larry.

"What's this all about?" Vockler demanded, in arms length of them now. "C'mon, let's hear it!"

"Hell's sakes, I can see it stickin' outa his pocket!" scowled Rodd, pointing.

"You're loco," protested Stretch.

He reached to his hip pocket and tensed.

"Just freeze, you hear?" ordered Vockler.

"*Freeze!*" He whisked the wallet from the taller drifter's hip pocket and showed it to Trenkler. "This is yours?"

"Damn right," nodded Trenkler. "Go ahead and check, Sheriff. It's got my initials inside. B.T."

"Deputy," corrected Vockler. "I'm Deputy Sheriff Miles Vockler."

"If you're a *smart* deputy, you ought to be able to smell a set-up," Larry said grimly.

"Shuddup, you!" retorted Vockler. He checked the wallet and passed it to Trenkler. "Right. Good enough for me. Your property — in the scrawny galoot's pocket. He robbed you sure enough."

"Told you," said Rodd.

"Now, just a doggone minute," growled Stretch.

"No back-talk — you're under arrest," announced Vockler. "Plain enough this other jasper's your partner, so I'm takin' both of you in. This shotgun's cocked — both barrels — so no tricks. Slip them holster thongs, unstrap your weapons and hand 'em to him." He nodded to Rodd. "Careful now. One funny move and . . ."

"*You* be careful," countered Larry, eyeing him coldly. "I'm gettin' the idea you're a mite too eager, Vockler, just *cravin'* to blast us."

"I got the same feelin', runt," muttered Stretch.

With the muzzles of a shotgun inches away, neither Texan would turn foolhardy. Larry said, as he began disarming himself, "Every man in the place is watchin'. They're all witnesses, Vockler. If your trigger-finger does somethin' stupid, they'll bear witness we weren't resistin'."

"Don't preach law to me!" snarled Vockler.

Stretch followed his partner's example, slipped his holster thongs, unbuckling his buscadero with extreme care, then passed his belted .45s to the leering Rodd, all the time wondering, 'Where've I seen this hombre before?'

When Rodd was hefting both gunbelts, Vockler said triumphantly, "You two'll follow us to the county jail. I'll need your statements."

"Our pleasure," declared Trenkler. "And I hope they get what's comin' to 'em."

"Count on that," chuckled Vockler. "I'm gonna have evidence aplenty to hold 'em for the circuit judge. They'll have their day in court, and then it's a state pen for 'em. Now move out, tall men, and you better remember I'm right behind you and this thing stays cocked till you're in a locked cell."

"A real sorehead," Stretch remarked to Larry. "I bet this is the most fun he's had since last time he picked his nose."

"I think you're right," said Larry.

"Move!" roared Vockler.

In such circumstances, the veteran trouble-shooters could tight-rein their anger, if not their contempt. After making their exit, they were ordered to turn into the alley beside the saloon. Vockler was not yet ready to advertise his big coup. He intended summoning Henry Bryar, editor of the Gilmore County *Dispatch*, to the county jail tomorrow morning. Until then, he would savor his victory and the indignation of his famous prisoners. This was better than he had wished for. A saloon brawl would have sufficed, the Texans in the thick of it. But Emerson a lousy pickpocket! So much for their great reputation, their fame as defenders of the rights of honest frontier folk. Bryar would have no option but to listen to his account of this affair and print it, giving him due credit for apprehending the living legends. Everything comes to he who waits!

So the prisoners, their captor and their accusers weren't seen in the brightly-lit main street. Vockler took them to the rear door of the county jail via the long alley paralleling Main Street at its east side. Before unlocking the door, he passed his shotgun to Trenkler and ordered him to keep it pointed at the Texans.

The snoring Elmer Walley was dead to the world in the nearest single to the back door. He didn't rouse when the men moved along the passage and

Vockler unlocked and opened the door to a two-bunk cell.

"Now," he growled. "Empty your pockets. Drop everything on the floor — then I'll search you."

The prisoners were forced to surrender every item, not just their small change, their jack-knives and Larry's wallet containing their bankroll; their tobacco and matches too. Ordered into the cell, they made for the bunks, seated themselves and watched the deputy secure the door. Vockler then retrieved his shotgun from Trenkler, uncocked it and led them along to the office.

When he heard the connecting door close, Stretch muttered in disgust, "He sure did it slick — the bastard that slipped his wallet in my pocket. I didn't feel a thing."

"He's an expert," said Larry.

"The other one — I could swear I've seen him someplace, and recent," scowled Stretch.

"Me too," nodded Larry. "Didn't look so tidy at the Ortner claim, the day we dumped Kaye there. I only caught a glimpse of him, but I'm as sure as you."

"Him that planted his wallet on me . . . " began Stretch.

"We never saw him before," said Larry. "But he has to be one of 'em. Chances are he was spyin' on Cosmo's claim that time." He swore softly. "Plain enough why they set us up. We gave 'em a bad time when they tried to ambush us. Or they know who we are and don't crave to trade lead with us again. But, right now, it's Vockler I'm frettin' about. He'll cost us a lot of hours, amigo. When them wagons roll tomorrow mornin', they'll roll without us. We'll be stuck here with just one hope."

"What hope?" asked Stretch.

"The other deputy — or their boss the sheriff — got more brains than Vockler," said Larry, "'less they're Texan-haters too. And I don't want to believe that."

"You think Vockler knows who he's

arrested?" Stretch grimaced helplessly. "Yeah, that could be it. Damn fool looked *too* happy."

After locking his prisoners' personal effects in the office safe, Vockler ordered Rodd to hang their weapons on the gunrack, seated himself at Kelland's desk and urged the complainants to describe exactly what had happened at the Branding Iron.

"Tell it slow, and one at a time," he muttered inking a pen. "I got to get it all down on paper, then you'll read and sign your statements, and that'll do fine for the circuit-judge."

The hard cases repeated their lies and, when the deputy had written down every word, signed the statements. Vockler, with relish, added his own signature.

"That's all, sir?" asked Rodd.

"Plenty," grinned Vockler. "You're free to go."

"We sure won't linger in this town," mumbled Trenkler, still into his role of resentful victim. "Fine thing when a man can't buy himself a drink without some trail-bum stealin' his wallet."

He and Rodd left, he to check out of the room and board place and collect an empty, tightly-rolled grainsack, Rodd to go find Merrill. The night was young. Before making their next move, they would have ample time for boosting their courage with something stronger than coffee.

Gleefully, Vockler helped himself to one of his boss's cigars, lit it, placed the statements on the blotter and used the ashtray as a paperweight. He then rose, opened the cellblock door and sauntered arrogantly along the passage to gloat over his catch.

The Texans stayed seated when he stared through the bars at them.

"You don't look so high and mighty now," he jeered. "I know who you are, you smart-ass show-offs."

"We *know* you know who we are," drawled Larry. "That's why you're near jumpin' for joy."

"Valentine and Emerson — real hot

shots — heroes," leered Vockler. "And I nailed you, but good!"

"Runt, I think he's so blame happy he'll wet his pants," said Stretch.

"Could happen any second," agreed Larry.

"Keep it up," invited Vockler. "The sassy back-talk, the foolery. *I* get the last laugh!"

"Not you, Vockler," frowned Larry. "Us. We ain't thieves and you know it, unless you hold no file on us."

"Oh, we got a file sure enough," chuckled Vockler. "Big fat file full of bulletins and newspaper cut-outs and . . ."

"Read it again," scowled Larry.

"I've read it a hundred times and it makes me sick to my stomach," Vockler said defiantly. "Always figured you show-offs ain't as do-good as folks think, and now I've proved it. I got you cold."

"For pickin' pockets?" challenged Stretch. "C'mon, feller, you know better."

"We'll talk to your boss," decided Larry.

"Off duty," said Vockler. "Won't be comin' in till after breakfast-time — about the same time I'll be sayin' my piece to the jasper that runs the newspaper here."

"So, meanwhile, we have to send a message to a gent stayin' at the Sherwood Hotel," said Larry.

"I'm no messenger-boy, Valentine," Vockler was stone-walling and loving it.

"Get word to a lawyer then," said Larry. "We're entitled, and we got cash enough for . . ."

"In the mornin'," grinned Vockler.

"Hell, we got to be out of this town manana — early!" fumed Stretch.

"No chance," was Vockler's parting thrust.

Feeling ten feet tall, he turned and hurried away to lock the jailhouse door and resume his patrol, leaving the Texans cursing.

"It couldn't be a reasonable badge-toter," fretted Stretch. "Had to be a mean-brain like him, a bum that's hated us from way back."

"Cosmo'll think we've quit on him," said Larry. "Unless he asks around and finds out what happened."

"You think, when the sheriff shows, you can talk us out of here?" asked Stretch.

"Give it my best shot," muttered Larry. "But, by then, the rigs could've left, could be miles east of here." He loosed another curse. "You know what the worst of it is? The worst of it is, if I can convince the sheriff it was a set-up and he sets us free, I can't clobber that fool deputy. You bust a lawman's jaw, you're back in the can again."

"I can understand that disappoints you some," Stretch sympathized. "Vockler's a hombre *ought* to have his jaw busted."

When Heenan relieved him at midnight, Vockler deliberately refrained from mentioning his arrest of the notorious trouble-shooters. And, when the Texans failed to show up at Tucker's the freighters waxed philosophical.

"Maybe Larry got into an all-night poker party," suggested Erling.

"Makes no never-mind," shrugged Worth. "We don't need 'em to spell us, what with Gibb's place close by, a stablehand on duty and a lawman patrollin'. You bed down in a wagon, Whit. I'll come wake you when I need some shut-eye."

Two and a half hours after midnight, with the saloons closed, the town was tomb-quiet and Steve Heenan checking doorlocks several blocks away from the Sherwood Hotel. For Ortner's men, it all seemed ridiculously easy. The window of the ground floor rear in which the girl slept had been left half-open; the atmosphere had been humid when she retired.

She was fast asleep when Merrill and Trenkler raised the window and climbed in. In the back alley, Rodd sat his mount and held the reins of the other horses, watching both extremities of that long laneway. The blow swung to Mary Kate's head by Merrill, after he raised her to a half-sitting position, guaranteed she would not regain consciousness till she and her abductors were out of earshot of the town's southern outskirts. Trenkler unrolled the sack and pulled it over her head and shoulders and down to her feet. Merrill raised her, waited for Trenkler to climb out, then passed her through to him. He followed, after placing the sealed envelope on the dressing table.

With Rodd's horse toting a double load, the bundle draped behind him and tied down, the three made a quiet exit from Gilmore's Ford. Somewhere uptown, Heenan heard the faint sound of receding hoofbeats, but thought nothing of it.

In the clearing, Pitch heard the horses and hurried to the north edge of the timber. He returned a few moments later to announce, "They're comin' back."

"Could you see . . . ?" began Ortner.

"They got her," grinned Pitch. "Bundle on Jesse's horse has to be her."

"Not yet," Ortner chided Darrow, who was about to kill the fire. "I'll tell you when."

Rejoining their cohorts, Merrill and his companions bragged it had all gone well. The Texans were in jail, and seizing the girl had been no problem at all.

"She's comin' around," chuckled Kaye, hearing a muffled groan.

"Muzzle her," ordered Ortner.

The hostage was dumped by the fire and the bottom of the sack untied. Rodd gripped the girls' bare ankles while Trenkler tugged the sack free. She lay there in her flimsy nightgown and groaned again, but with her eyes closed. Rodd used two bandanas, balling one and ramming it into her mouth, wrapping the other about the bottom of her face and knotting it behind her neck.

"We're all set, huh?" said Boneen.

"Put her into the sack again and secure it to a horse," muttered Ortner. "Remember, when we reach our next position, she'll be conscious, so we use the hoods again. We'd have to silence her — permanently — if she saw our faces, and I can't bargain with Coote by trading a dead hostage. Everybody get mounted." He nodded to Darrow. "Now you can put out that fire."

When they were all mounted, Merrill reminded him, "The bridge is north."

"Too risky," said Ortner. "We'll ride due east from here and find an alternate fording place."

Around 7.45 a.m., Cosmo Coote rose, bathed, dressed and descended to the hotel lobby. The night-clerk would be relieved a quarter-hour from now; he yawned and nodded to the old man. Cosmo looked to the dining room entrance, grinned sheepishly and remarked, "Didn't mean to sleep so late. Guess my niece and the tall boys're eating already."

"I haven't seen her yet," said the

clerk. "She'd still be in her room. The tall men . . . " He squinted at the register, glanced behind him to the keyrack and shrugged. "Mister Valentine and his friend didn't use their room it seems."

"They're still out?" frowned Cosmo.

"Must be," said the clerk.

"Well, I better go rouse Mary Kate," Cosmo said impatiently. "We got to be travellin' again soon's we eat."

He moved into the downstairs corridor to knock at the door. From inside, silence. He tried the knob. It turned and he opened the door and entered.

7

'Count On Us'

FOR a long moment, Cosmo stared at the rumpled bed, the open window, the closet with its door half-open, revealing his niece's dumped Levis, blouse and jacket and, hung with loving care, her new gown. The new shoes and her boots were on the floor beside the bed. His disquiet increased when his gaze strayed to the dressing table and the envelope propped against the mirror. He moved across for a closer look. His name was hand-printed on it in pencil.

His hands shook as he tore the flap and extracted the folded sheet, squatting on the edge of the bed. Ortner's demand was unsigned and, like his name on the envelope, printed in pencil. He read it with his heart heavy, the ugly taste of fear and defeat in his mouth.

'Stay steady now,' he chided himself. 'You can't help her by fallin' apart.'

He restored the message to its envelope and pocketed it, rose and began stowing his niece's personal effects and clothing into her faded and frayed carpetbag. While he was doing that, he heard a familiar 'whuff'. He glanced to the window. Rufe had managed to jump up to the sill from outside. Now the shaggy mongrel perched there, yawning; for him it had been a busy night.

"Hope you enjoyed yourself, consarn you," growled Cosmo. "If you'd been close — where you belong — it couldn't've happened."

Rufe plopped to the floor, plodded to the bed and found the strength to leap onto it. He rummaged, sniffing at the sheets and the pillow, whimpering uneasily, then fixing his brown eyes on Cosmo in mute appeal.

"We're gettin' out of here," mumbled

Cosmo. He quit the room, closed the door and set the bag down. Rufe sat by it while he hurried upstairs to collect his own gear and don his hat. When he came down and picked up the bag, the hound followed him to the lobby. The day-clerk was on duty now. "I'll settle up. How much for the little lady, me and Valentine and Emerson?"

"They paid when they checked in," the day-clerk reminded him. While accepting payment for the two singles, he said affably, "Hope you folks enjoyed your stay."

"Thanks," sighed Cosmo. "We're sure obliged."

Heavy-hearted, he trudged to Tucker's with Rufe at his heels. The teams were in harness, his mount and Mary Kate's and the mule tied behind the second rig and the freighters grim-faced this morning.

"Where's the little lady?" asked Worth.

"Tell you later," frowned Cosmo, staring around. "How about Larry and Stretch?"

"Got bad news for you, Cosmo," said Erling. "A little while ago, a feller came by to talk to Gibb. He was in a saloon last night where — the damnedest thing happened."

"A lot of bad things're happenin'," Cosmo said shakily. "Go on, tell me."

"A deputy arrested them Texas boys," muttered Erling. "Seems some jasper's wallet was lifted and they claim Stretch did it. They're both in the county jail, Cosmo."

"Aw, hell!" groaned Cosmo. He bowed his head, pondered this second reversal a moment, then dropped the carpetbag. "Put that in a wagon and wait for me. I got to go talk to 'em before we pull out." Before leaving, he glared at the dog. "You stay put!"

Rufe cringed. The old man made for the county jail. He resisted the urge to run. How long had it been since he could do that? The years were catching up on him. He was distraught, oblivious to his hunger, trying in vain to calm himself.

After his hitch at midnight to dawn patrol, Heenan had gone home to sleep. Vockler had slept on the office couch and was now bathed and shaved and eagerly awaiting the editor of the *Dispatch*, having ordered a passer-by to summon him. He was at the Justin stove, fixing coffee when Cosmo trudged in without knocking, to be appraised disapprovingly.

"Pardon me all to hell if you were expectin' some other feller," growled Cosmo.

"What d'you want, old man?" demanded Vockler.

"Here to visit with your prisoners, meanin' Valentine and Emerson," announced Cosmo. He unstrapped his sidearm, placed it on a desk and spread his arms. "Want to make sure I ain't hidin' a weapon, a hacksaw maybe? Check me over, then let me in there."

"They ain't allowed visitors."

"Who says so?"

"*I* say so."

"You the sheriff?"

"I'm Deputy Vockler."

"All right now, Deputy Vockler. Is it the sheriff's rule I can't talk to your prisoners — or just yours? Maybe I should go find the sheriff. Where's he at right now?"

Vockler swore impatiently. Cosmo took the envelope from his pocket, held it firmly and spread his arms again. The deputy made short but thorough work of frisking him, then grudgingly unlocked the door to the ground floor cell-block. As Cosmo crossed the threshold, he told him, "I'll be lockin' up after you. Knock when you're through — and make it a short visit, hear?"

When Cosmo appeared at their cell door, the tall men quit their bunks and crossed to him, alarmed by his expression. He clutched at the bars.

"Listen now, Cosmo, we were set up," muttered Stretch. "You know we ain't thieves."

"Sure as hell you were set up, and

here's why!" The old man shoved the envelope at Larry. "They got Mary Kate! That's all I found in her room! It was empty — 'cept for all her duds. Them buzzards took her away in nothin' but her wore-out nightgown."

Larry swore bitterly and slipped the sheet from the envelope. The message read:

'IF YOU WANT THE GIRL RETURNED ALIVE, CONTINUE EASTWARD. TELL THE LAWMEN NOTHING OF THIS. AT A PLACE OF MY CHOOSING, WE WILL TRADE. THE GIRL — ALIVE — IN EXCHANGE FOR THE GOLD, THE WAGONS AND TEAMS.'

He passed the paper to his partner and traded stares with Cosmo.

"You got to do like the note says," he declared.

"I know it!" gasped Cosmo. "It's her life — she's got it all ahead of her. All the gold in the world ain't worth spit compared to her. She helped me mine it, Larry, every last piece of it, but it don't mean a thing now. Better her and me stay poor, just so long as she stays alive."

Stretch mumbled a curse and returned the note to Larry, who returned it to the old man.

"You're thinkin' we've failed you," he said.

"No." Cosmo leaned against the bars and shook his head. "Like you say, you were set up. No way you could guess it'd happen."

"Thanks, but we're blamin' ourselves just the same, Cosmo," growled Stretch. "Most times, we can smell a set-up. This time we . . . " He grimaced angrily. "Hell, runt, we're slowin' down."

"No we ain't," retorted Larry. "Cosmo, you'll be leavin' without us, but that don't mean you've seen the last of us. We'll get out of this calaboose. If we have to break jail, that's what we'll do."

"I don't see how you can . . . " began Cosmo.

"We'll be out of here, one way or another," Larry promised. "Won't try to catch up with you. What we'll do is hunt sign of the bunch that grabbed Mary Kate and tail 'em."

"If they spot you, it'll go bad for her," fretted Cosmo.

"You got our word," said Larry. "We'll be thinkin' of her every minute and we'll bird-dog 'em careful."

"Count on us," said Larry.

"We're good at that, old timer," Stretch assured him.

"Count on us," said Larry.

"We'd have to track 'em down even if they didn't have Mary Kate," Stretch said grimly. "We've been set up before, Cosmo. Any sonsabitches do that to us, they don't get away with it."

"Yeah, all right boys," muttered Cosmo. "But I meant what I said. Her life — all the gold in the world ain't worth me riskin' her life."

He turned, moved back to the jailhouse door and knocked. Vockler hurried to open up for him, ordered him to pick up his sidearm and get out, then resumed his seat at the sheriff's desk. Seated opposite him now was a portly, cigar-puffing local in town clothes topped off by a battered derby, Henry Bryar, editor of the Gilmore County *Dispatch*. The old man left without sparing Vockler's visitor a glance.

"Now, where was I?" The deputy leaned back in his boss's chair and rested his boot heels on the near edge. "Oh, sure. I was tellin' you how them no-accounts tried to give me an argument."

"I can understand that," Bryar nodded. "Considering who they are, the two you call no-accounts."

"You ain't takin' notes," Vockler complained. "You're supposed to write down what I'm tellin' you."

"Later — maybe," said Bryar.

"What d'you mean — maybe?" demanded Vockler.

"It's all a little inconsistent," Bryar said mildly. "Did I say a *little* inconsistent? Deputy Vockler, picking pockets is just not their style. If they're Valentine and Emerson . . ."

"That's who they are, damn it, no mistake," growled Vockler. "Wouldn't *I* know, me that's read our file on 'em time and time again?"

"Any reports in your file say they've ever been convicted on a theft charge?" asked Bryar. "Come on now, I'm as familiar with their rep as any other newspaperman. We know those hellers. We have our own records."

"I got 'em cold," insisted Vockler. "Hell, the man's wallet was right there in Emerson's hip pocket."

"I'm not doubting that," shrugged Bryar. "Listen, how about you start again. I want to hear exactly what happened in the Branding Iron, what was said, how the Texans reacted, one detail at a time."

"Knowin' they were in town, I was naturally leery of 'em, so I kept 'em under observation . . ." began Vockler.

He was still talking and the *Dispatch*

editor's pencil and notebook were still in his pockets when the sheriff at last arrived. Kelland entered, traded nods with Bryar and, as he hung up his hat, stared hard at Vockler. The deputy promptly vacated his boss's desk and transferred himself to the stool to the left of the cell-block entrance.

"'Morning, Dave," said Bryar.

"Henry." Kelland nodded again as he sank into this desk-chair. "How've you been, and what brings you to my office this fine morning?"

"Miles sent for me," said Bryar. "Made an important arrest last night he tells me." He jerked a thumb to indicate the cell-block. "Holding a couple of prisoners, real celebrities."

"That a fact?" frowned Kelland.

"They ain't as noble as some fools say," gloated Vockler. "Statements right there on your desk."

"Who're we talking about here?" Kelland asked, as he donned his spectacles. Vockler mouthed the names with relish. Kelland tensed, darted a glance at him, then read the statements. His face clouded over. Not his eyes. They gleamed, reflecting his anger. "Ever see them before, the two who swore these charges?"

"Strangers, and I don't care a damn," grinned Vockler.

"That's true enough," Kelland said coldly. He removed his spectacles and traded stares with the newspaperman. His gaze fixed on Vockler again. "You *wouldn't* care a damn, Vockler. You got what you've hungered for, or so you believe, an excuse for locking up those fiddlefoots you've hated for years."

"I've tried to warn him, Dave," said Bryar.

"He wouldn't listen to you, but he'll listen to me — if he hopes to keep his badge," scowled Kelland. "Vockler, you're a jackass with a heavy chip on your shoulder and you aren't thinking straight. You got their bankroll in the safe?" Vockler nodded sullenly. "They're not exactly broke?"

"I stopped tallyin' what's in Valentine's

wallet when I got to five hundred," muttered Vockler.

"So they can afford to retain a lawyer!" fumed Kelland. "They claimed the complainant's wallet was planted on Emerson?"

"I wouldn't expect they'd admit he's a pick-pocket," said Vockler.

"You took these statements, had the strangers sign them, then let them leave," Kelland guessed. "Damn you, Vockler, you *know* Valentine and his partner aren't thieves. That's on their record. If the strangers had sworn they saw those drifters rustling J-Bar stock, robbing the poor-box at the Baptist church or cutting my wife's throat, you'd *still* have arrested them, you wouldn't stop to *think*!"

"Fortunately for my health, I'm as sceptical as you, Dave," said Bryar. "It'll be a cold day in hell when I'm foolish enough to claim Valentine and Emerson are petty thieves — in print."

Kelland rose and paced, all the time

glaring at the now-intimidated deputy.

"They're shiftless and rowdy," he muttered. "They brawl, they gamble and they ramble. They have no respect for the law, but less for outlaws. They hate thieves and killers, Vockler, more than *you* hate *them*. A real lawman should no know better than to be jealous of them . . ."

"Just because they've been fighting outlaws for almost twenty years," grinned Bryar. "And always winning."

"Jealousy's a weakness — and spite is worse!" Kelland raged at Vockler. "You've checked our file on those trouble-shooters and hated everything you read, because you couldn't find one current warrant, one mean little excuse for apprehending them. Then a couple of strangers plant a wallet on them and cry 'thief' and you fall for it!"

"Now you know why I didn't take notes," Bryar told the deputy. "My readers wouldn't believe it, Dave doesn't believe it, I don't, and neither would Circuit-Judge McWhitty."

"You're orderin' me to turn 'em loose," Vockler said in acute misery.

"I'm ordering you to sit in your own chair at your own desk and to keep your mouth shut," retorted Kelland. "*I'll* attend to this. Unlock the door, unlock the safe too and put their stuff on my desk — then sit and stay quiet."

Moments later, he was walking the jailhouse passage, jingling a keyring, anticipating a storm of abuse from the occupants of the double cell. But there was no outburst. They got up from their bunks when he reached the cell door. Larry asked impatiently, but not aggressively.

"You the sheriff here?"

"David Kelland," he nodded. "Sheriff of Gilmore County." He fumbled for the right key. "Never thought, would never have believed there'd come a day I'd be apologising to you tumbleweeds."

"That mean you're beggin' our

pardon?" drawled Stretch. "On account of your sorehead deputy can't savvy a set-up when it's right under his nose?"

"Them hard cases lied," growled Larry. "And Vockler bought their lies."

"You already pegged him for a sorehead, so you know he believed what he *wanted* to believe," muttered Kelland. He unlocked and opened the door. "Understand now, I don't approve of your methods. Your record I approve — you've put many a badman where he belongs — but not your methods. I'm doing this because it's well known you have — uh — certains standards. With better than five hundred dollars in your bankroll, I'm not fool enough to believe you'd foul up your reputation by picking pockets. If you'll come along to my office, your property will be returned to you, then you'll be free to leave."

The tall men donned their stetsons and followed him to the office. Ignoring Bryar and Vockler, they moved straight to the gunrack and to retrieve and strap on their sidearms. Kelland identified the newspaperman, who addressed them cautiously.

"Will I bring Lone Star wrath on my head if I enquire what brought you to Gilmore's Ford?"

"I was about to ask that," said Kelland.

"Little escort chore," Larry said offhandedly. He and Stretch moved to the sheriff's desk to transfer their other effects to their pockets. When their hands touched their Bull Durham, they automatically began building smokes. "The freight rigs."

"I recognized them as Strachey wagons, saw them rolling on my way here," frowned Kelland. "Must have been purchased from that Cooper City outfit. I read something about pots and pans on the canvas and the drivers looked like peddlers."

"They're friends of ours is all," said Stretch. "And we were eastbound anyway. Ready, runt?"

"Ready," nodded Larry. Before following his partner to the street door, he turned to cold-eye Vockler and muttered a warning. "If we're ever in this town again and some lyin' skunk tells you we're horse-thieves or cardsharps, get the drop on *him* with your shotgun and step far clear of us. That way, you won't make a damn fool of yourself."

Quitting the sheriff's office, they beelined for Tucker's. Stretch moved on from there to collect the few items left in their hotel room, leaving his partner to saddle their mounts and secure their heavier gear. While Larry was thus occupied, Gibb Tucker came to him to remark, "The old feller looked plenty worried when he left with Oley and Whit."

"Old men fret a lot," said Larry.

"I didn't see the girl," frowned Tucker. "The mutt, but not her."

"Rode on ahead most likely," shrugged Larry. "Kid likes to hunt."

"I guess you didn't break jail,"

decided the livery-owner. "Otherwise the street wouldn't be so quiet."

"Pea-brained deputy name of Vockler made a dumb mistake," said Larry.

"Oh, Miles Vockler." Tucker nodded knowingly. "I've said it a hundred times. He'll never be as smart a lawman as his boss or the other deputy."

A short time later, mounted, the Texans were reading sign, or trying to, in the alley behind the hotel. More than a few locals had walked by since the girl was kidnapped.

"Flip a dime," Larry urged impatiently. "We know they took her east, but which end of town did they leave from north or south?"

Stretch obliged.

"Tails."

"Bueno, we start checkin' south. If we cut no sign, we circle round to the north."

South of Gilmore's Ford, riding slowly and well separated, they scouted for tracks. A hundred yards of open terrain they scouted, and then Stretch's whistle alerted Larry; he turned the sorrel and rode to where his partner sat his pinto. Stretch pointed to the ground.

"Three critters. I figure one of 'em's totin' double. She don't weigh heavy, the little lady, but that's how I read it. And these tracks lead to the timber south."

They followed the tracks to the timber and moved boldly through to the clearing; it didn't take brilliant deduction to assure themselves Mary Kate and her abductors were far east of here by now.

The ground of the clearing, the hoof and boot prints, blackened patch and half-burned matches and cigar and cigarette stubs told them plenty.

"They didn't linger," said Larry. "Broke camp right after the three from town arrived with Mary Kate. Two of 'em'd be the hombres that bulled Vockler into arrestin' us."

"Eight in all," opined Stretch. "Them with the hoods, same bunch ambushed us. And Ortner and his crew'd be a safe guess."

"Now comes the tricky part," Larry said as they urged their horses to the east edge of the timber. "Now we got to bird-dog 'em and make damn sure they don't spot us."

"Remember the note?" drawled Stretch. "They won't be fearin' a law-posse tailin' 'em."

"Nor us," scowled Larry. "We're supposed to be stuck in the county jail."

Cosmo had held back from explaining his niece's absence till the wagons were several miles from the county line and the freighters spelling their teams. Erling dropped from the second rig and came forward to stand by his partner and the old man slumped beside him. Cosmo told it then, slowly, in faltering sentences.

Erling rid himself of a half-smoked cigar and did some fast and fancy cussing but, out of deference to Worth, was careful not to blaspheme.

"The evil men do — they pay for," Worth grimly intoned. "In the next life, if not in this."

"Larry and Stretch, they'll do their doggonedest," sighed Cosmo. "But it mightn't be enough. They mightn't get out of that jail-cell in time. Thing is boys, when them thieves stop us, we're gonna have to do what they want, turn over my fortune, these rigs and teams too, to get Mary Kate back."

"They hold all the aces," complained Erling.

"Gold will not protect them from the Lord's punishment," muttered Worth.

"All the years we been haulin' freight, Oley, this'll be the only time we've given in to bandits, let 'em take everything," said Erling. "But what in tarnation else can we do? It's the kid's life."

"I don't care about the gold no more," mumbled Cosmo. "She's the only kin I got and deserves her chance to live her three score and ten. So we got to do it."

"So be it," said Worth. "We move on soon as the horses're rested."

The dog joined them — hesitantly. His whimper, the look in his brown eyes, were eloquent.

"Poor little critter's missin' his purty boss," observed Erling.

Cosmo relented, climbed down and bent to pat the furry head; his hand was licked eagerly.

"No use me blamin' you, Rufe," he said softly. "You weren't by her on account of you had yourself quite a night doin' what comes natural. Reckon she'll forgive you, little feller."

Would Rufe forgive himself? That was another question.

* * *

Her captors had taken precautions. When they nightcamped, she was relieved of her gag, but blindfolded. Only then did Ortner and his men remove their hoods. At his nod, Merrill addressed the girl harshly.

"You set quiet till we're through eatin' and maybe we'll feed you, might even give you a blanket so you won't freeze. Try takin' off that blindfold and you'll get the back of my hand, you hear?"

Her head had stopped aching. She was apprehensive, but determined to show no fear.

"I hear you," she growled. "What a pack of heroes. Huh! Two-legged coyotes is what you are."

"You'd be buzzard-bait, girlie, if you wasn't so valuable," growled Boneen. "You're the end of the rainbow for us."

"I don't know what you're jawin' about," she mumbled.

"If you ain't guessed, you're plenty stupid," grinned Pitch. "The old man's gonna turn it all over to us, the gold and the wagons to haul it. That's how he gets you back."

"Uncle Cosmo'd *never* do that!" she gasped.

"Wanta bet?" chuckled Kaye.

Ortner pantomimed instructions. One man watched the hostage while the others set about fixing a cookfire and rigging a picketline for the horses.

"Lookouts?" asked Merrill.

Ortner drew him aside and spoke quietly; he was determined the captive would be unable to identify him by his voice, could not recall if they had ever met, but was loath to take chances. Merrill dropped his voice when Ortner insisted lookouts be posted.

"The boys're saddlesore and brain-tired. We *need* lookouts up here? Coote didn't dare talk to the sheriff and there's no way them trouble-shooters could get out of that jail. Who'd be huntin' us?"

"With a fortune almost in our grasp, we can't afford to relax our vigilance," muttered Ortner. "Damn it, Clay, if that doesn't make sense to you . . ."

"Yeah, okay, whatever you say," shrugged Merrill. "Leon and Boyd'll set watch after we eat. Two-hour hitches all night."

Mary Kate was allowed to feed herself, but blindfolded, one of the men warning that, if she pulled that bandana down, she would be at once shot. She feigned resentment while eating by feel but, in fact, the warning raised her hopes of surviving this ordeal. If she couldn't identify them, they would eventually release her, confident she could not offer descriptions to the lawmen to whom her abduction would be reported.

She ate to keep her strength up and, while eating, tried to make sense of it all. How much could she remember? She had a clear memory of retiring, relishing the comfort of her bed at the Sherwood Hotel. Must have fallen asleep almost immediately. After that — what? A raging headache and acute discomfort and steady movement, muffled voices, one voice raised in a curt command. No names, that one had warned. They had to be — the word used was 'anonymous', but she didn't understand it's meaning. As her head cleared and she regained her sight, she realized she was secured to a horse, draped in front of its rider. She could raise her head just enough to see one of two of her captors, but not their faces; they wore hoods. Just before first light, a halt was called to spell the horses and, before she could look around, somebody covered her eyes with another bandana, knotting it behind her head like the one securing her gag.

After that, more movement. With no light filtering through her blindfold except at intermittent intervals, but the morning sun easing her chill, she could figure they were staying clear of open areas, travelling whatever cover they could find. No pause for lunch. They travelled all day, ending their journey with a long climb to this place. A mesa? The top of a high hogsback?

She would be rescued, she assured herself. By now, Larry and Stretch would be searching for her, and they would do it right. This was her big hope. These women-stealers craved the gold; they had made that clear enough. But, soon enough, those trail-wise Texans would catch up with them. No Double C gold for this wolf-pack. Just bullets.

In the hour after midnight, the Texans were sheltering in a semi-circle of rocks to the west of the ridge atop which their quarry was nightcamped. Far to the west, the boulders tall enough to conceal the sorrel and pinto as well as their owners. They wore their ponchos with blankets draped over the ponchos; it was cold, but they weren't betraying their presence by making a fire.

Their gaze was directed to the fireglow atop the ridge, Larry using his field-glasses.

"Long ways off," Stretch commented. "But we can get closer when we have to. A lot of brush 'tween here and the ridge. Them things any use at night?"

"Not as good as in daylight," muttered Larry.

"You seein' anything?"

"Enough. It's them all right. I keep catchin' movement. Must be some hombre passing this side of the fire. Safe bet they posted lookouts."

"We wait it out, huh?"

Larry lowered the glasses. They squatted, drank whisky and chewed jerky.

"The layout's just right for 'em, but for us too," said Larry. "We know the regular trail's a ways north of us and them. High grass all the way from the ridge to the trail 'cept for a patch of timber, not a big patch. I don't reckon they'd try signalin' the freighters from the ridge. More likely, when they sight the wagons, they'll come down, keepin' the timber 'tween them and the trail."

"When they move, we move," guessed Stretch.

"But careful," frowned Larry.

"Uh huh, careful," agreed Stretch. "They got Mary Kate."

"All they'll be thinkin' of are the wagons and what's in 'em," opined Larry. "We'll be movin' through the brush and, 'less we get unlucky, they won't know we're around till we're close enough to score on 'em. Don't ask me how long we'll have to wait."

"Well," shrugged Stretch. "Like we been sayin' all along, them rigs roll slow and steady. That's no passel of chicken feathers they're totin'."

"They left this mornin' right after Cosmo visited with us," mused Larry. "Right now, they'd be camped somewheres west of here. Maybe they'll show manana — some time manana."

At first light, while his partner opened a couple of cans of pork and beans, the field-glasses gave him a clearer view of the ridge-top. Smoke spiralled to the sky. The kidnappers would account for a hot and hearty breakfast. Would they think to feed their hostage? Were they keeping their hands off her?

While they were eating, Stretch read his mind.

"Runt," he said softly, but vehemently. "If this deal's gonna end with a shootin' showdown, them polecats don't rate an even break — any kind of chance."

"Hell, no," agreed Larry.

And, having eaten, they looked to the loading of their weapons.

8

The Gold, The Girl And The Guns

IT was 11 a.m. when Ritchie Boneen lowered the telescope, retreated to where his cohorts sat by their saddled horses and announced, "They're comin'."

"How far?" Ortner demanded, getting to his feet.

"Quite a piece west and rollin' slow," said Boneen. "We got time aplenty."

"Cover up," ordered Ortner. "Then remove the girl's blindfold."

Mary Kate sat tense in the flimsy, threadbare nightgown, her only covering. When Merrill untied the blindfold, she blinked against the sunlight. It took her a few moments to focus on her captors, hooded, wearing dusters or slickers, all eight of them.

"Now we make for the timber," guessed Kaye.

"Now," nodded Ortner, and growled a reminder to Merrill. "You're in charge of the hostage and you're our spokesman. You know what to do and say. We aren't negotiating. You'll relay my demands — and that'll be that."

Larry was using his binoculars again, scanning the terrain west and sighting distant moving dust when his partner calmly reported, "They're on the move."

"Bueno," grunted Larry. As they got mounted, he grinned wryly. "What're you waitin' for? Say it like you always do."

"Here we go again," drawled Stretch.

"And easy does it," said Larry.

While the hooded horsemen descended to the flats two abreast, the Texans nudged their mounts clear of the rocks and made for the screening brush. They were holding to their hunch the opposition would await the coming of the big rigs in the stand of timber between the ridge and the trail and were bent on reaching the east edge of the brush. From there, Larry anticipated they would see and hear the challenge.

Fifteen more minutes and, perched beside Worth on the seat of the first wagon, Cosmo stared ahead and mumbled, "Could happen purty soon."

"They plan on tradin', we're movin' toward as good a place as any. We're easy to see from them trees up there right of us or from farther southeast, that woody ridge."

The hijackers were in the timber now, Ortner passing the word they would make their play when the wagons came level with this vantagepoint. And the trouble-shooters were watching from the east edge of the brush, their Winchesters unsheathed and ready for action.

The wind was blowing from the south. Rufe, curled up till now by the tailgate of the wagon driven by Erling, suddenly whimpered, rose on his hind legs with his forepaws atop the tailgate and raised his nose. He sniffed, made a low growling sound, then whimpered. Rising higher, he scrambled over the tailgate, dropped to the trail and scuttled into the high grass south of it. Erling didn't note his departure, nor did Cosmo or Worth, all three staring ahead. But Stretch reached for his partner's arm and gripped it.

"Runt . . . !"

"What?"

"I only spotted him for a second, but it's him for sure. Rufe."

"Where?"

"He's into the high grass now. You can't see him from here."

"Damn!" breathed Larry. "If he starts yappin' . . . "

"Which he's liable to do when he sights his boss," frowned Stretch.

"Nobody should sell a dog short," muttered Larry. "Wind's comin' in from south. You can bet your double-cinched saddle he's caught scent of her." He watched the timber and the slowly approaching wagons. "Well, they got instincts. If he can sniff her, he can sniff danger too."

"Passable smart critter, Rufe," reflected Stretch. "Maybe he's one hound-dog knows when he oughtn't yap."

Only they could speculate on the dog's position, how far he had advanced through the high grass. Cosmo and the freighters were unaware he had taken off, and the horsemen in the trees had eyes only for the wagons.

"They're almost level with us," Ortner observed to the only man not sitting his mount. "Do it now."

"Right," nodded Merrill.

Moments later, Cosmo shuddered and pointed.

"Look there!"

"I see 'em," growled Worth.

He hauled back on his reins and Erling followed suit. The two figures were clearly visible, one of them easily recognized, Mary Kate, barefoot and stumbling, a hooded man gripping her left arm and holding a pistol to her head. The girl and the hooded man moved across the thick-grassed flats till they were in earshot of the stalled vehicles. Then, in a line, seven hooded riders emerged from the timber and advanced, one leading Merrill's horse.

"That's right, you heroes," muttered Larry. "Get well clear of them trees. Keep thinkin' you're bossin' this deal, callin' the plays. I want you wide open — when the time comes."

"Real nervous set-up," complained Stretch. "We daren't buy in while ever he's got a gun at her head."

Merrill paused. Behind him, the riders reined up.

"Let her go!" cried Cosmo.

"Read the note, didn't you?" challenged Merrill. "Her life for the gold and the rigs, straight trade! You or the drivers make a wrong move, I blow her head off!"

"Sonofabitch," mumbled Erling.

Merrill stated terms.

"First thing, shuck the hardware!

I want to see every weapon on the ground — fast!"

"We have to do it, Whit!" Worth called to Erling.

Rifles and shotguns were tossed to the ground and followed by the belted and holstered pistols.

"I see two saddle-animals and a mule!" yelled Merrill. "Climb down — this side — untie 'em and mount up! Then you head straight north!"

"Mary Kate . . . !" protested Cosmo.

"I let go of her when you're far clear of the wagons!" shouted Merrill. "You can wait for her a quarter-mile north! She'll make it on her own two feet! That's the deal — and there ain't a damn thing you can do about it!"

"You're lower'n a snake's belly," panted the girl.

"Shuddup, brat," growled Merrill. He raised his voice again. "Old man, you got two choices!"

"The hell he has!" Erling retorted. "You're givin' him *no* choice!"

As they urged their horses another ten yards forward, Ortner calmly assured his men, "It's working. Coote and the drivers are about to climb down. There'll be no more argument."

Worth bellowed a challenge.

"We got no guarantee you'll turn the girl loose!"

"You're gonna have to take our word for it!" Merrill was out of patience. "C'mon, we're through parleyin'! Get down off of them seats!"

"Maybe I can get a bead," Stretch said yearningly.

"At this range, you'd be riskin' her life," complained Larry. "His gun's at her head and he's too damn close to her."

"I won't wait!" warned Merrill.

And, slowly, Cosmo and the freighters quit the wagonseats and climbed down. Ortner's hood masked a triumphant smile. He had planned well. His big moment was at hand.

Mary Kate, sickened by memories of muscle-strain and callouses, all the effort it had cost her and her uncle to mine and cache their fortune, was assessing her chances of turning the tables. Could she do it, turn fast, knock the pistol upward before it discharged, ram a knee into the gunman's crotch and wrench the gun away from him? If she succeeded, Uncle Cosmo and the drivers might take advantage of such a distraction, drop flat, retrieve their fallen weapons and open fire; they wouldn't hesitate on her account, not if she threw herself to the ground.

Now or never, she was thinking, and on the point of making her move, when Merrill loosed a howl of pain. The Texans saw it too, the dog rising beside the gunman, biting into the calf of his left leg and hanging on. Merrill shook that leg frantically, Rufe clinging tenaciously, fangs sinking deeper into flesh, and the girl reacted violently, twisting, grasping the wrist of the hand holding the gun, forcing the muzzle clear of her head.

"That's it!" growled Larry, as if

Stretch needed telling.

They heeled their mounts and broke cover, charging out of the brush cavalry-style, rising in their stirrups with their Winchesters barking. To the accompaniment of a chorus of oaths, the seven hooded men swung their weapons to sight on their challengers, while Erling dropped flat to crawl to his fallen rifle and urged his partner and Cosmo to do likewise. They obeyed, but Cosmo mumbled anxiously, "She could get hit! We daren't get to shootin' 'less she ducks!"

Responding to Larry's yelled advice, Stretch veered to race his pinto to the struggling couple. Mary Kate's left arm was free. Now she gripped Merrill's wrist two-handed, exerting all her strength to keep the six-gun pointed skyward, while he howled in agony and fury with pain shooting up his leg and tried to bend and strike at the dog with his free hand.

Already, Larry had emptied a saddle. The horses of the other riders milled, nickering shrilly over the din of barking rifles and booming Colts. Fast-triggered slugs whined past Larry, coming dangerously close, but he continued his charge, sighting and firing with deadly accuracy.

Reaching Mary Kate and the struggling man, Stretch eased his pace but did not rein up nor reverse his rifle. He brought the barrel down hard on Merrill's headgear, the impact denting the crown of the hat and plunging Merrill into oblivion.

"Grab ground, honey!" he ordered, wheeling his mount.

Rufe finally let go. The girl dropped flat with the dog huddled beside her, and Cosmo and the drivers promptly chose targets from prone positions.

A slug scored a shallow crease between Larry's left elbow and shoulder, numbling his arm. He swore in frustration, but now his partner was rejoining the fray, Winchester raking the hooded riders now beginning a retreat to the timber. Larry dropped his rifle, drew his Colt and cut loose, toppling another horseman. Bullets sped past Stretch and he automatically changed direction, alerted by the racket of riflefire from beside the wagons; Cosmo and the freighters were buying into the action.

None of the four unscathed riders made it to the timber. One almost took the taller Texan's life; the bullet in fact rendered Stretch hatless and singed his hair. That man, firing over his shoulder, missed with his next shot, Stretch's rifle barked again and the slug knocked him out of his saddle. It was anybody's guess who — Larry, Cosmo, Worth or Erling — downed the other three, who pitched from their mounts, hitting the thick-grassed ground and staying down.

Larry reined up and called to Cosmo and the drivers to cease fire.

"You're leakin' blood, runt," warned Stretch.

"Think I don't know it?" scowled Larry. "I got pain, but the arm's workin' again. We got chores, so let's get to it."

Stretch sheathed his rifle and drew a Colt. The trouble-shooters dismounted and, not for the first time in their hectic career, did what had to be done, moved warily among the scattered dead and wounded. Soon enough, they knew they'd be delivering only two live prisoners to the law officers of Gilmore's Ford. They removed the hood of the unconscious and haggard Trenkler, traded glances, then replaced it.

Mary Kate rose with Rufe in her arms, happily licking her face, when they reached Merrill. While Stretch removed the unconscious man's hood and hat, Larry studied her and felt his fury flare again.

She looked so pitiful, hugging the dog, her begrimed face lit by a smile of gratitude and relief.

"Knew you and Stretch'd come for me, Larry."

"Did they . . . ?" he began.

"Must've beat me on the head when I was sleepin'," she said. "They sure handled me rough, but you made 'em pay."

"Did they . . . ?" he began again.

"No," she said. "Wasn't none of 'em thought of — you know. Only thing on their minds was our gold."

"Use your rope," Larry urged Stretch. "This polecat'll come to his senses 'fore we see Gilmore's Ford again, so truss him good. I'll hogtie the other one." He dropped his gaze to Merrill's ugly, still bleeding leg-wound, then patted Rufe's head. "You done good, ol' buddy. Too bad you couldn't go for his no-good throat."

"You don't have to get your purty feet cut, honey," offered Stretch, after unhitching his lariat. "Straddle my mount and hustle on back to your Uncle Cosmo."

"Tell him to stay put," said Larry. "We'll be along in a little while."

After the girl eagerly accepted this offer, the Texans set about securing the dead and wounded to horses. They did expose a face or two, but then replaced the hoods, only did this to confirm Larry's hunch as to their identity; he was determined the losers would be delivered to the Gilmore County law looking as they had looked when their spokesman bellowed their demands to Cosmo. The sack in which Mary Kate had been transported out of town was used to carry their sidearms.

Larry found and sheathed his rifle. They led the laden animals to the stalled wagons and shook their heads to Cosmo's speech of gratitude. Stretch drawled a reminder.

"You gents did your share."

"Little lady's in the rig, gettin' dressed," said Erling.

"The evil men do sure brings 'em down," Worth grimly declared, eyeing the death-horses.

"We're takin' 'em back to Gilmore's Ford, Cosmo," said Larry. "I don't want this outfit to go on without us, because Stretch and me like to finish what we start. What I want you to do is just move the rigs off the trail and make camp — and wait for us."

"Be glad to do that," frowned Worth. "We're still a fair piece from Cooper City. You and your partner took care of one wolf-pack but, if we got raided again . . ."

"We'll all feel safer with you boys along," Cosmo said fervently.

"Talked your way out of jail, huh?" grinned Erling.

"We figured the sheriff couldn't be as knuckle-headed as the deputy that arrested us," shrugged Stretch. "*No* man could. Trouble was, we had to sweat it out in that jail till the sheriff showed."

"Dave Kelland," said Worth. "Good man."

"With a brain in his head — which helps a lot," remarked Larry. "Now, we'll get back to you soon as we can. Meanwhile, rest your critters, fix yourselves some chow and just wait."

"Won't mind the waitin', son," said

Cosmo. "Never did figure on reachin' Cooper City any special time."

He handed Larry the envelope containing the demand pencilled by Ortner. A short time later, watching the tall men lead the eight laden horses westward, Erling chuckled harshly and predicted to his companions, "Gonna be some red faces in that town when them Texas bucks show up again."

There *were* red faces, the morning Larry and Stretch returned to Gilmore's Ford tagged by eight horses toting six dead and two wounded, all hooded. Henry Bryar's was red from his exertions; after bounding out of his office, he trotted wheezily beside the Texans' horses, trying to gasp out questions while keeping pace. The east and west sidewalks were soon crowded by gaping townfolk. Following the approach of the grim procession from the porch of his office, Sheriff Kelland coloured angrily. But, predictably, Miles Vockler's face was the reddest of all, when he emerged from the office and recognized the tall men.

"Damn it, Valentine," Kelland challenged as they reined up.

"I'll tell it in your office," offered Larry. "And we don't mind if the scribbler hears what I got to say. You'll need a doc for two of these bandidos. All the others need is an undertaker. Sooner they're underground the better."

Kelland called orders to locals who hurried to obey. The death-horses were led away, after which the Texans untied the wounded men and toted them into the office.

"You gonna just stand there gawkin'?" Stretch asked the fuming Vockler. "Move your ass, unlock a cell and dump these galoots."

"You'd better have a good explanation for this," warned Kelland.

"And I want to hear it!" Bryar panted as he trudged in and made for a chair.

"C'mon now," Larry chided Kelland. "You know our style. Would we bring in six stiff and two live skunks if we'd busted any laws?"

"Well . . . " began Kelland.

"My ol' buddy talks clearer when his throat ain't dry," drawled Stretch, glancing about. "You got a bottle here? And another deputy?"

"A smarter deputy than Vockler?" prodded Larry. "One that can pour us a shot without spillin' good liquor on your floor?"

"Lock up those men, then have somebody fetch a doctor," Kelland ordered Vockler. He sighed heavily as Vockler dragged the wounded into the cell-block. "All right, Valentine, I'll play barkeep while you heroes rest from your labors."

"They've done it again," mumbled Bryar, producing notebook and pencil.

The Texans drew chairs up to the sheriff's desk and seated themselves. Vockler emerged from the jailhouse and, from the street doorway, impatiently ordered a passer-by to summon a doctor. From his private bottle, Kelland poured shots of bourbon for the trouble-shooters, the newspaperman and himself; he didn't feel like buying his senior deputy a drink right now.

When he sank into his desk chair, Larry led off by passing him the ransom demand and inviting him to read it.

"Then," he offered, "I'll name the bastard that put them words on paper. You'll get your explanation — in spades."

Kelland sipped bourbon, read the demand and passed it to Vockler.

"How much gold?" he asked, having regained his composure.

"Not all that much," lied Larry. "But enough to tempt a sonofabitch name of Ortner." He went on to recount events preceding the Coote party's arrival in Gilmore Ford, Cosmo's suspicion that a spy had discovered his cache before being scared off, the ambush that had backfired, then the scheme that had succeeded here and might have resulted in Ortner's acquisition of the cargo, but for Kelland's agreeing he and Stretch had been victims of a set-up. "Don't mean to brag," he continued. "But it's safe bet some of Ortner's bunch recognized us, remembered we're bad news for hijackers and didn't hanker to trade lead with us again."

"Couldn't afford for us to be in that hotel — we had a room a little way along from Mary Kate's — when they grabbed her," explained Stretch. "We sleep light."

Larry jerked a thumb toward the cell-block.

"One of them losers in there, he's the hombre claimed my partner lifted his wallet," he said. "You knew we were set up, and now you know why."

"My other deputy, Steve Heenan, worked the graveyard shift that night, and last night, which is why he's sleeping now," frowned Kelland. "He's reliable, but it's a big town. If he'd been anywhere near the hotel, there'd have been no kidnapping. He must've been at least three blocks away. All right, let's hear the rest of it. You trailed the kidnappers after I released you?"

He listened to it all. So did Bryar, his pencil busy. Bluntly, Larry described the final confrontation, he and Stretch in hiding and watching, waiting their chance to foul up the exchange, the girl for the gold, but as helpless as Cosmo and the drivers until the intervention of a mongrel devoted to his mistress and proddy enough to distract Merrill in an extremely painful way. Rufe was accorded his due of credit and the ensuing gunfight recounted offhandedly.

The doctor arrived. Kelland greeted him and eyed Vockler enquiringly.

"Doc'll be safe enough," the deputy mumbled. "I left the door unlocked. They're too weak to make a break."

"Go in, Doc," urged Kelland. "Leave the jailhouse door open, Vockler." He watched the Texans drain their glasses. "That's all of it?"

"And — uh — you aren't objecting to my running the story just as you've told it?" Bryar asked eagerly.

"Can't stop you from doin' that, scribbler," muttered Larry. "But there's one part of it you better not leave out."

"We wouldn't take that kindly," warned Stretch.

"Just tell me which part," invited Bryar.

"The trick they pulled to get rid of us, to make sure we couldn't stop 'em from grabbin' the girl and tradin' her for the gold," growled Larry. "Valentine and Emerson ain't sneak-thieves. They don't pick pockets. If you forget to tell how this boneheaded deputy fell for that cheap trick, couldn't wait to hustle us into jail . . . "

"We'd be plumb disappointed," Stretch said softly. "And, when we get disappointed, we turn real mean — savvy?"

"Rely on me," soothed Bryar. "That point will be stressed. The integrity of the Lone Star Trouble-Shooters is beyond question. They would never descend to such dishonesty. They hold all thieves — from petty thieves to rustlers and hold-up artists — in contempt."

"Just don't forget," said Larry.

"I won't," promised Bryar.

"Nothing more to say?" asked Kelland.

"That's all of it." said Larry.

"All right." The sheriff set a pad on his blotter and inked a pen. "I'll summarize your statement and ask you to read and sign it. It won't be necessary for you to remain here till those two in the jailhouse stand trial. You are, of course, eager to rejoin the wagons and escort them to Cooper City."

"Got a few things to pick up here, then we'll be on our way," nodded Stretch.

"Write fast," urged Larry.

"Mind your mouth," scowled Vockler. "You're talkin' to the sheriff."

Larry retorted, while eyeing him scathingly, "And lookin' at the littlest man in this territory."

"Listen you . . . !" gasped Vockler.

"Leave it at that!" Kelland said sharply.

Vockler lapsed into silence; he was sulking.

A few minutes after the sheriff was through with them, the trouble-shooters startled the proprietress of a ladies' store by confronting her and declaring they wished to buy female underwear.

"Not for us," Stretch hastened to assure her. "And — uh — she's about so tall, about this wide across her hips — beggin' your pardon — and lean where she buckles her belt."

"We'll get her a purty hat too," Larry decided. "Skirt and a blouse and maybe some sweet-smellin' soap."

When the Texans crossed the bridge and took to the trail again, their gifts for Mary Kate were neatly parcelled and, rather than crumple them into their saddlebags or packrolls, they toted the parcels in the crooks of their arms. And Rufe had not been forgotten. Bulky in the gunnysack hanging from Larry's saddlehorn were two items obtained from the kitchen of the Sherwood Hotel. Bones. Big ones.

These tokens were accepted gleefully by Mary Kate and Rufe when the Texans rejoined the wagons. She cooked and dished up a substantial meal, after which the journey east was resumed.

Cooper City was reached early afternoon of a sunless day, the sky overcast, but the threat of a storm could not depress Cosmo Coote or his niece nor, for that matter, the Texans or the freighters. They were accorded a warm welcome by Ed Strachey, who was on Main Street when they arrived.

"Stall the rigs in front of the bank while I send for Sheriff Pooley," he urged. "We're gonna do this right. Whit, you tell the bank staff to get ready to open the vault and make room for an important delivery."

The trouble-shooters helped unload the gold and, in the bank, watched it being transferred to the strongroom by the freighters and two cashiers. An assayer had been summoned, had fetched his equipment and was making ready to perform his task. He also fetched sandwiches; it promised to be a lengthy chore, a professional valuation of so sizable a quantity of gold.

Larry rolled and lit a cigarette and watched the operation soberly. His arm-wound was healing, one of many he had suffered over the years, his partner also. So many close calls, so many *too* close, requiring surgery during which the Grim Reaper had hovered, only to be thwarted. He and Stretch were still alive, still a threat to the lawless, and sometimes he thought it a miracle, wondered how much longer they could last.

"You're thinkin' about the Ortner bunch," guessed Stretch. "The hell with it, runt. Them or us. What could we do? Just watch and see 'em trade the little lady for all this gold? We couldn't do that."

"No," agreed Larry. "We could never do that."

"All over now," shrugged Stretch.

"You want to linger in this burg a couple days or hit the trail again? Nothin' to hold us here."

"Check into a hotel, buy supplies tomorrow mornin' and head on out," decided Larry. "Cosmo's got a good and important friend here, so he don't need us no more. I figure Strachey and the banker'll send his cash to Kansas City or Saint Louis, wherever he settles, the safe way. What they call a bank draft, somethin' like that. Sure, Cosmo and Mary Kate got nothin' to worry about from here on."

When all business at that bank had been finalized and the cash value of the cache estimated Cosmo and his niece traded incredulous stares.

"What'd you expect it'd tally to?" Strachey good-humoredly challenged. "Ten — twenty thousand?"

"I didn't figure . . . " mumbled Cosmo.

"Called it your fortune, didn't you?" grinned Strachey. "And a fortune it is. Whatever big town you settle in — and I predict you'll decide on Saint Louis — you'll be one of its wealthiest citizens." He clapped a hand to Cosmo's shoulder and added, "It couldn't happen to a better man."

At his insistence, the whole party repaired to his private office for a preliminary celebration. Glasses were filled and he toasted and congratulated Worth and Erling, Cosmo and his elated niece and, in particular, the Texans, after his employees recounted their two run-ins with the Ortner gang.

"Without Larry and Stretch . . . " Cosmo said wistfully.

"Yeah," nodded Erling. "The hijackers would've won, Ed. No question."

"I know you by reputation, gentlemen," Strachey remarked to the tall men. "To you, it was nothing new or different, right? Nothing you haven't done before?"

"We don't look for all this gun-trouble," muttered Stretch. "It's just somethin' keeps happenin' to us."

Larry, seated with Rufe perched on

his lap, drawled a rejoinder.

"Somethin' that'll happen again soon enough."

"I call it plain crazy," protested Mary Kate. "We could make you rich, but you just won't let us pay you for . . ."

"Mucho dinero means a happy future for you, honey," Larry told her. "For us, it'd mean bigger trouble than we ever had."

The trouble-shooters said their good-byes then and there. By 10 o'clock of the following morning, they were gone from Cooper City, headed 'no place in particular'.

THE END

Books by Marshall Grover in the Linford Western Library:

BANDIT BAIT
EMERSON'S HIDEOUT
HEROES AND HELLERS
GHOST-WOMAN OF CASTILLO
THE DEVIL'S DOZEN
HELL IN HIGH COUNTRY
TEN FAST HORSES
SAVE A BULLET FOR KEEHOE
DANGER RODE DRAG
THE KILLERS WORE BLACK
REUNION IN SAN JOSE
CORMACK CAME BACK
RESCUE PARTY
KINCAID'S LAST RIDE
7 FOR BANNER PASS
THE HELLION BREED
THE TRUTH ABOUT SNAKE RIDGE
DEVIL'S DINERO
HARTIGAN
SHOTGUN SHARKEY
THE LOGANTOWN LOOTERS
THE SEVENTH GUILTY MAN
BULLET FOR A WIDOW

CALABOOSE EXPRESS
WHISKEY GULCH
THE ALIBI TRAIL
SIX GUILTY MEN
FORT DILLON
IN PURSUIT OF QUINCEY BUDD
HAMMER'S HORDE
TWO GENTLEMEN FROM TEXAS
HARRIGAN'S STAR
TURN THE KEY ON EMERSON
ROUGH ROUTE TO RODD COUNTY
SEVEN KILLERS EAST
DAKOTA DEATH-TRAP
GOLD, GUNS AND THE GIRL
RUCKUS AT GILA WELLS
LEGEND OF COYOTE FORD
ONE HELL OF A SHOWDOWN
EMERSON'S HEX
SIX GUN WEDDING

Other titles in the Linford Western Library:

TOP HAND
Wade Everett

The Broken T was big. But no ranch is big enough to let a man hide from himself.

GUN WOLVES OF LOBO BASIN
Lee Floren

The Feud was a blood debt. When Smoke Talbot found the outlaws who gunned down his folks he aimed to nail their hide to the barn door.

SHOTGUN SHARKEY
Marshall Grover

The westbound coach carrying the indomitable Larry and Stretch headed for a shooting showdown.

FIGHTING RAMROD
Charles N. Heckelmann

Most men would have cut their losses, but Frazer counted the bullets in his guns and said he'd soak the range in blood before he'd give up another inch of what was his.

LONE GUN
Eric Allen

Smoke Blackbird had been away too long. The Lequires had seized the Blackbird farm, forcing the Indians and settlers off, and no one seemed willing to fight! He had to fight alone.

THE THIRD RIDER
Barry Cord

Mel Rawlins wasn't going to let anything stand in his way. His father was murdered, his two brothers gone. Now Mel rode for vengeance.

ARIZONA DRIFTERS
W. C. Tuttle

When drifting Dutton and Lonnie Steelman decide to become partners they find that they have a common enemy in the formidable Thurston brothers.

TOMBSTONE
Matt Braun

Wells Fargo paid Luke Starbuck to outgun the silver-thieving stagecoach gang at Tombstone. Before long Luke can see the only thing bearing fruit in this eldorado will be the gallows tree.

HIGH BORDER RIDERS
Lee Floren

Buckshot McKee and Tortilla Joe cut the trail of a border tough who was running Mexican beef into Texas. They stopped the smuggler in his tracks.